MOUNTING DEUCE

ADDISON WINTERS

Mounting Deuce
~ the Heat of Arrest series ~
Book 1

Addison Winters

Copyright 2019 ADDISON Winters

 Created with Vellum

INQUIRIES ABOUT ADDITIONAL PERMISSIONS

SHOULD BE DIRECTED TO:
ANGELA@SCARLETTINKPUBLISHING.COM

Cover Design by Mad Hat Designs
Edited by Charlene Burgett

ISBN 978-1-948143-12-7

Library of Congress Control Number: 2019909025

ACKNOWLEDGMENTS

I'd like to thank Linda Russell and her wonderful team at Forward PR & Marketing for taking the reins and running with them. Plus, Shari Ryan at MadHat Books for her creative genius in designing my covers. Also, Cheryl Monette, Charlene Burgett, and Melinda Rueter for your incredible insight and feedback. You all helped to shape and develop my words. I love you all!

Finally, I'd like to thank my amazing, loving, and supportive husband, Eric; without whom none of this would have been possible. You are my everything!

For the original Detective Deuce ...

ONE

THE SUN WAS BEGINNING ITS decent behind the desert mountains filling the sky with a brilliant collage of orange and gold fire. I glanced at the GPS on my dashboard and made the next left-hand turn. The queasy feeling in my stomach made it difficult for me to recall why I was even doing this.

"I'm going home." I announced to Shelly whose voice was ringing through the speakers in my car.

"No, you're not. Who knows? He might be fabulous." I could hear the wittiness in her voice.

"I can't believe you made me join Match." I complained once again.

"You work all the time and never go out. You need to rejoin the dating world."

"Says you." I muttered. "I can't believe you're making me do this." I snickered without humor.

"It will do you good. You're too damn picky. You could find something wrong with no matter what Saint asked you out!" She snickered.

"I am not picky." I fired back. "I'm selective." I reasoned.

"Besides, my Prince Charming got hit by a bus when he was a child."

"Good grief." Shelly chuckled. "Are you there yet?"

"Yes," I pulled my car down the long entryway to the golf resort. "This place is gorgeous."

"Where are you at?"

"Ocotillo Golf Club and Resort in Chandler." I rattled off the sign as I passed by.

"What the hell are you doing way out there?"

"I have no freaking clue. This is where he told me to meet him."

"Dump him now. That's too far to drive." She stated.

"This was your idea, remember. Besides, maybe from your place, but it's fifteen minutes from mine." I reminded her.

"Him living out there disqualifies him automatically. I'm trying to get you over to my side of the city, not further away from me."

"Like I said, this was your idea, not mine."

I turned pulled into a parking spot near the front and turned off the engine. "I don't want to do this." I said again.

"Have fun and call me later with the details." Shelly chuckled. "And be nice!"

"Yeah, right." I muttered and opened my car door, ending my conversation with her.

I took a deep breath and decided to leave my golf clubs in the car for a moment. I didn't want to lug them around when I didn't even know where I was going. The early June evening air was stifling as the temperature clung near the triple-digit mark. It was going to be another miserably hot summer in Phoenix.

I walked across the parking lot thinking about getting back in my car when I spotted Dylan walking towards me. There was no backing out now.

"Hi, Arya." He embraced me briefly. "Did you bring your clubs?"

"Yes. I left them in the car." I nodded over my shoulder.

"Okay. Well, let's get them." He smiled warmly.

We walked towards my car, and I noticed he was maybe an inch or two taller than my almost 5'6" stature. I tried not to chuckle recalling him saying he was 5'10". I always found it humorous how some men were so insecure about their height. But I did notice he had beautiful blue eyes and a striking smile that was offset by a chiseled jaw. His short brown hair stood up in little spikes on top his head in a cute boyish manner. He was very nice looking.

We retrieved my clubs, and I walked back up to the clubhouse. Dylan already had his bag out on the driving range and was talking a mile a minute about his former modeling career. He even took out his phone to show me a shirtless and buffed photo of himself back in the day. I tried to act impressed and not to visibly roll my eyes. His confidence came out more like arrogance.

I nodded along appropriately and began hitting some balls on the tee. Dylan stood there for a few minutes carefully studying me.

"You realize you're standing all wrong, don't you?" I hadn't.

"Oh. Sorry."

"Keep your back straight and bend your knees a bit more." He walked up behind me. "Like this."

Dylan wrapped his arms around me, pressing his body close to mine. He placed his hands over mine.

"Interlock your fingers like this." I did exactly what he did and gripped the club. He placed his hands over mine. "And when you swing, keep your left arm straight and follow through like you're pivoting." He moved my body like his puppet "Now, you try." He stepped back out of my way.

I followed his instructions to the letter and hit the best drive I've ever done.

"Much better." He smiled.

"Thanks!" I grinned back.

After several more attempts, Dylan approached me again from behind.

"No. Like this." He demonstrated in the same fashion as before.

I could feel his body pressed up against mine. His chest and abdomen were solid beneath his dark fuchsia polo. His breath was hot on the back of my neck. I felt him move in a bit closer as his hips pressed against mine.

God, let that be Chapstick in his pocket.

I could only hope.

But as he shifted his weight through the swing, I could tell it wasn't.

Damn. That sucks!

The sun slowly sank behind the mountain as the golf balls disappeared into the orange sky. I was trying to concentrate on my swing and thinking how impressed Shelly was going to be on Sunday morning. I was notoriously bad at golf, and according to Shelly, my forty years of softball experience had severely hindered my game.

Dylan continued to ramble on about his work with the Special Olympics and various charitable organizations he was involved in. I wasn't sure if he was being truthful or not, but if he was, he was certainly going for sainthood.

As we slowly lost light and the groundskeeper made his presence known behind us, nudging us off the range, Dylan was kind enough to clean off my clubs and walk me to my car.

"What would you think about having a glass of wine on a boat tonight?" He asked as I shut my trunk.

"That would be wonderful." I admitted as I wiped my brow.

"I live on a lake around the corner and have a pontoon sitting on the dock outside my back door." He smiled deviously. "We could cruise around the lake with a bottle of wine." He raised an eyebrow.

I debated for a moment and trusted my gut feeling about Dylan. He may be an arrogant narcissist, but overall, he was harmless.

"I would like that."

"You're telling me that you would get in my truck and go with me to my house after you've known me for two hours?" He paused and studied me carefully making me feel very self-conscious.

"I trust my instincts, and I can follow you in my car." I smirked.

"You really shouldn't do that." He set his clubs down beside my car. "It could be dangerous."

I wasn't sure if I felt cocky or just perturbed by his cockiness – and lack thereof.

"Are you dangerous?" I smirked.

"No, I capture criminals." Dylan smirked back.

"Huh?" I raised my eyebrows at him. "Don't tell me you're a fucking cop." I sighed heavily.

Damn it!

One of the two professions I swore I'd never date. I have a great deal of respect for law enforcement officers and firemen, but I never wanted to sit at home and wonder if my spouse was going to make it home in one piece.

"A Lieutenant actually." He said proudly.

I tried not to roll my eyes at his confidence.

"Are you still on patrol?" I knew very little about how rankings and such worked in law enforcement.

"Yes, but I used to be in Vice. You can Google my name on

YouTube, and it'll bring up some of the news media interviews I've done on cases I've worked." He boasted.

"Cool." I tried to act enthused. "I thought you worked with the Special Olympics." He had spent a good twenty minutes an hour ago bragging about his work with children with disabilities and showing me pictures of him putting medals around their necks on the podiums.

"I do. But it's all volunteer." Dylan explained.

"I see."

"So, how about that drink?"

"Okay," I shrugged. "I'll follow you."

I climbed back into my car as he walked across the lot with his truck. I turned over the engine, and as soon as the car sprang to life, I asked Siri to call Shelly.

"Wow, that was quick. Was it that bad?" She answered on the second ring.

"I'm going to kill you!" I put my car in reverse and followed Dylan's truck out of the lot.

"What'd he do?" She laughed.

"One, he's a fucking cop! Two, he was pressing up against me trying to instruct me on my golf swing and let's just say the golf pencil was bigger ... and thicker."

"Oh, no!" Shelly laughed even harder. "I'm sorry!"

"No, you're not." I turned left at the light behind Dylan.

"How was I supposed to know he's a cop. It wasn't on his profile." She exclaimed. "But you can look at it this way, at least you know he has his own set of handcuffs and knows how to use them." She could barely contain herself.

"You're such a bitch." I chuckled.

"It's a shame your date ended so early. That sucks."

"Who said it ended? This is intermission." I accidentally snorted.

"I thought you were in your car."

"I am. I'm following him over to his place. He's got a pontoon on the dock outside his back door. We're going to cruise the lake with a bottle of wine." I said with sarcasm.

"La-di-da." I could picture her rolling her eyes.

"He's trying to be impressive. He rambled on and on about his pontoon, his speedboat, his motorcycle, his convertible, his truck, and his house on the lake." I droned on indicating how unimpressed I was.

"Wow, guess he is overcompensating, huh?" He giggled.

"From what I could feel pressed against my ass, he needs to." I confessed. "Oh, and he lives in a gated community." I stated as I pulled up behind him at the gate and waited while he punched in his code.

"On a cop's salary? He must have family money." Shelly stated.

"Or he's on the take." I reasoned cynically.

"Just be careful." She cautioned. "Oh, and you're following him, right?"

"Yeah."

"What's his plate number, just in case you turn up missing."

I rambled it off to her as I pulled into his driveway beside her. I said goodbye to her and quickly got off the phone as Dylan walked up to my car.

"See, I told you it was practically around the corner." He smiled.

"I didn't even know any of this was tucked away back here."

"It's my own little oasis. I love it."

Dylan's home was a ranch style house with a three-car garage that looked fairly new. I couldn't tell the exact color because it was too dark, but from what I could see by the courtyard lights, it was more of a cornflower blue and grey. The courtyard was beautifully decorated, and unlike anything I was expecting.

He unlocked the front door and turned off the alarm. We

were immediately overrun by an excited Pitbull mix that jumped up on each of us.

"This is Rex." Dylan petted the solidly built dog roughly, yet playfully. "He's a big baby."

"He's beautiful." I scratched his head as he jumped up on me.

"Get down, Rex. She doesn't want you on her clothes." He pushed the dog down.

The foyer opened into a huge living room with a cathedral ceiling. It was breathtaking. I could not have imagined his place looking like this. I was shocked.

I followed him into the kitchen and great room area. His home looked like something out of country Home and Garden magazine. It was simply gorgeous with all its hardwood floors, custom cabinets, and colors in faded blues, smoky greys, and rustic brick. I was astonished by how immaculate it was. I was in love.

With the house, not the man...maybe the dog!

It had to have been decorated by his ex-wife. I have never met a heterosexual man with such style. I could be wrong, but not in my personal experience.

Dylan took me on a tour of the place, and each room was as elegant as the next. It was unbelievable. I had not encountered many men with such an incredible homestead. I had no clue what the Phoenix PD paid their officers, but I was pretty sure he was either mortgaged to his boxers or came from family money.

Rex and I followed Dylan back into the kitchen where he fixed us a Rum and Coke. He was yammering on about all the improvements he'd done on the house since his ex-wife moved out two years earlier. He claimed to have done all the decorating himself.

I scanned around the family room and kitchen as we stood at the bar and wasn't sure if I believed him or not. Either way, it really didn't make a difference to me.

The three of us walked out onto the back patio. There was no backyard to speak up. It was maybe twenty-five feet to the water's edge. Dylan opened the gate on the pontoon and held out his hand to me. Rex scampered up after us and jumped into the captain's chair.

"He likes the boat." Dylan shrugged.

"I can tell." I giggled and took a seat across from him.

Dylan started up the pontoon and eased it out onto the open water. I relaxed back in my seat and enjoyed the warm breeze blowing through my hair. The temperature was still in the high nineties, but the night sky was enchanted with bright stars. It was romantic and peaceful.

"How long were you married?" I asked between sips.

"Which time?"

"You've been married more than once?" I raised an eyebrow at him.

"Yes, twice. Seven years the first time. Five the second." He lifted his glass to his lips.

"And no kids?"

"Nope. My first wife didn't want any and I did. My second wife had an affair with another woman and is now living with her."

"Oh." I wasn't sure what to say.

"And you just have the two?"

"Yes. My son is twenty-six and in the military. My daughter is twenty-three and goes to ASU. She lives with me."

"That's nice. And you've lived in Arizona a couple years now?" He asked.

"Three last February."

"Do you like it here?"

"It's different. I miss the green, but not the snow." I smiled.

We cruised around the lake and chatted casually about his job. He was a nice guy once he let down his guard and dropped the arrogant attitude. I wasn't sure if his rough exterior was a defense mechanism or if the rum and Coke were exterminating the bug up his ass.

Dylan tied the boat back up at the dock and escorted me into the house. I set my glass on the bar and picked up my purse and keys where I'd left them.

"Are you sure I can't interest you in another drink." He offered.

"No, but thank you. I still have to drive home." I paused, not sure what else to say.

"Yeah, I'd hate to get you into any trouble." He flashed a devilish grin.

"I guess the officers in this city are real assholes." I smirked.

"Only when provoked." He took a step forward and placed his hand on my arm.

Dylan drew me nearer to him and leaned in towards me. He kissed me gently. I could taste the rum on his lips. A small smile eased across his lips as his deep blue eyes caressed mine. I kissed him a little more firmly. His arms wrapped around me and pulled me against him.

With the sad reminder of the Chapstick in his pocket pressed hard against my pelvic bone, I took a step back.

"I really must be going." I exclaimed. "I have a 5:30 tee-off in the morning." I lied.

"Yeah, I have a busy day tomorrow too." He took my hand and led me to the front door.

"I had a really wonderful time this evening." Dylan opened the door for me.

"Me too." He leaned in and kissed me once again. "I'll call you this weekend. Maybe we can get together on Sunday or something."

"Sounds good." I embraced him and gave him another quick kiss before making my way to my car.

~

MY DAUGHTER, Brylee, arrived home from an evening out with the girls as I was getting out of the shower. I was wrapping my hair in a towel and sat down at my vanity.

"Hey momma, how was your date?" She flopped down across my bed.

"Fundamentally, it was the perfect date. We met at the driving range. He helped me with my swing. We had a drink and cruised around the lake on his boat. But the guy, not impressive." I summed up my evening for her. "How was your night?"

"Same ol', same ol.'" She rolled her eyes. "We went down to the Sandbar and had a couple drinks. Hanna broke up with her boyfriend, so we spent the night listening to her bash him. Thrilling."

"Exciting."

"So, what was wrong with the guy?"

"Arrogance for starters." I shook my hair out of the towel and turned to face her. "He was handsome. Sexy. Cocky." I started brushing my hair. "Oh, and a fucking cop." I snorted.

"Seriously? Ugh." Brylee brushed her long, chestnut hair out of her eyes. "But cops can be sexy. Remember Casper?" She giggled.

"Oh, right. Casper. Damn, he was the epidemy of a sexy cop." I agreed.

"And a little arrogance isn't all that bad." She shrugged.

"Yeah, but it wasn't the arrogance on him that was little." I raised my eyebrow at my daughter.

Our relationship had shifted in the last couple years to one of a close friendship as well as mother and daughter. She had moved with me after her father, and I got divorced, and while she still talked to him frequently, the divorce had strained their relationship. He was a topic I rarely discussed with her.

"You slept with him on the first date? Damn mom." Judgment rang through her voice.

"No. Of course, I didn't. Like I said, he was helping me with my golf swing. And in doing so, he was pressed up against me." I set my hairbrush on the vanity.

"Ouch. That bad, huh?" I lifted my little finger at her.

"I thought he had Chapstick in his pocket." I laughed. "It wasn't Chapstick."

"Poor guy." Brylee chuckled.

"It's sad cause he was so cute. Plus, he had this gorgeous home on the lake in this beautiful gated community. Not to mention all the freaking vehicles and boats. Worst of all, he had the coolest dog, Rex. I could have taken him home and spoiled him rotten."

"You cannot date a man for his dog, Momma." She smirked. "Didn't you say he was a cop?" I nodded. "How can he afford all that? I thought cops didn't make crap."

"They don't. He must have family money or something." I shrugged.

"Maybe he's on the take." She raised her eyebrows at me. "We are only two hours from the border."

"Nah. He's so straight and narrow, he squeaks when he walks." I explained. "He thinks too highly of himself to do anything unethical." I rolled my eyes at the memory of his endless 'me talk.'

"So, I'm guessing you won't be going out with him again." She climbed off my bed and walked over to me. "You do realize, momma, that someday you may actually have to go on that second date with someone." She leaned over and kissed the top of my head.

"Why? What's the point?" I made eye contact with her in the mirror. "It'll never last anyway."

"Not all men are like Dad, Momma." My daughter said in a low voice. "You're going to meet someone amazing someday. I promise." She smiled and gave me a gentle squeeze.

"Not on Match." I smiled.

"Give it a chance."

"Good night, sweetheart." I patted her hand before she headed to her own room.

TWO

I MET SHELLY FOR LUNCH the following Wednesday. She had chosen a Mexican restaurant inside an old church in the heart of Phoenix. She always enjoyed upscale and unusual places, and this was one of her favorites.

I had met Shelly a couple years ago when I'd first moved to Phoenix. She owns a small business with about fifty employees and was wanting to restructure it. As an organizational, industrial psychologist, with a small consulting firm, she contacted me for help. We worked together for more than three months, and now her revenue had doubled.

During that time, she and I had become good friends. Shelly was five years older than me and had a bit of a wild side in her. When we'd first met, she was in a twelve-year relationship with a man a decade younger than her. She had found out early last fall that the bastard, Matt, had been cheating on her for the last couple years. And sadly, he rarely worked as a mechanic and lived off her money in her home.

Shelly had been devastated. She had kicked him out, but in doing so put down the deposit on a new apartment for him and paid off his car. I couldn't understand her reasoning, but instead just listened to her vent and cry over him.

A month later she had decided to join Match and pestered me to join it with her. She claimed it was so I could view the profiles of the men she was interested in or who messaged her, but then she finally revealed that her ulterior motive was to get me back into the dating world as well.

And I had tried. I went out on several first dates, and so far, only one-second one. Aaron was a high school principal, nice looking, charming. We had a great first date, and a week later, he and I joined Shelly and her date, Brendon on a Sunday morning for 18 holes. It was disastrous.

Aaron spent the entire morning criticizing and critiquing everything I did. I was on my third mimosa in as many holes. As much as I dearly loved playing golf and enjoyed our Sunday tee-offs, I could not wait to be rid of him. It was the longest morning.

Aaron and I parted ways in the parking lot that morning, and I never saw him again. He tried to reach me several times, but I let his calls go to voicemail. By the end of the second week, he had given up.

That was my last date on Match before Dylan — six months later, and I knew already, there would be no second date.

"Hey, it's about time. You're late." Shelly informed me as I sat down across from her.

"Am not." I set my purse down on the seat beside me. "You said 12:30, and it's five of."

"Whatever." She picked up her menu. "I ordered you a Mai Tai and some queso dip. I'm starving."

"How's the diet going?" I smirked.

"Fuck you, bitch." She said with a smile.

"You love me."

"Keep telling yourself that."

The waiter came around and dropped off our drinks, dip, and

chips. Shelly immediately started snacking while I ordered a couple carnitas tacos. She ordered a steak burrito with refried beans.

"Have you heard from teeny weeny?" I wrinkled my forehead at her.

"Teeny weeny?"

"Well, calling him Chapstick lacks a certain poetry. Don't you think?"

"Needles. Short for needle dick." I chuckled. "Fits him perfectly."

"Such a shame. He's so cute."

"I know. But his arrogance was a bit much for me." Shelly shook her head in agreement. "Look at what he sent me this morning." I pulled up my text messages and handed her my phone.

"A gym pic? Seriously?" She looked at the photo again. "He's got a great body. It sucks he has no gun in his holster." She handed me my phone back.

"Even if he did, his personality is a bit much for me."

"Okay, so you move on to the next one. You have to kiss a few toads to find your prince." She shrugged.

"No, thank you."

"You can't give up now."

"Look, I'm not like you. I enjoy being alone. I've never had it before. It's kinda nice." I sipped my drink.

"You're too damn picky."

"It took me three years to get my freedom from that SOB, and I'm still fixing the damage he did. I never want to go through all that again." I explained.

"Not all men are like your ex."

"I understand that, but I'm not willing to take the chance."

"So, you're just going to give up on love?"

"I enjoy what I have with Ryan. I don't need anything else."

"You could have so much more with him if you'd simply let him in." Shelly cocked her head to the side and looked at me with judgment.

"Ryan is not the sort of man you have a relationship with. You know that." I reminded her.

"You mean, that you don't have a relationship with. Not me. Ryan's sexy as hell and you have so much fun with him."

"Fun. Yes. But anything serious? No."

"Fun can be good, Arya."

"I know that. But that's all Ryan is. He could never be more." I let out a deep sigh in exasperation.

"Why not?"

"Because as beautiful as he is to look at, as talented as he is in bed, and regardless of how much fun I have with him; I've had dinner with the man, and it was painful." I told her.

"Why? Did he not use the right fork?" She smirked.

"No," I laughed. "But the man is not exactly intellectual. I'm honestly surprised he can tie his own shoes." I picked up a chip and scooped up some queso before taking a bite. "Don't look at me in that tone of voice. I tried dating Ryan when I first met him."

"And you've pushed him away every chance you got."

"That's not true. I still see him."

"And when was the last time you saw Ryan?"

"I don't know. January. February maybe." I'd lost track.

"Yeah, it's a meaningful relationship." Shelly laughed.

"It's all I want right now." I told her.

"Whatever. I refuse to give up on love."

"You can't give up on something you don't believe exists." I mumbled.

"You're becoming cynical."

"And if this is all that is out there," I held up my phone with

Dylan's picture still on the screen. "I'll happily buy more stock in Duracell."

"I'm not giving up on you." She shook her head slightly at me.

"How is Brendon doing?" I tried to change the subject.

Shelly, a nervous eater, spent the next hour finishing two more drinks, emptying the queso, her plate, and snacking on the remainder of the chips while telling me she's decided to loan this man thirty-five grand to start a landscaping business. She rambled on about her reasoning and her feelings for him. I bit my lip and tried not to ask how someone so intelligent could be so dumb. She was an incredibly intelligent lady, but her low self-esteem made her a bum magnet for all worthless men.

"Say something." She finished off the last of her drink and waved to the waitress to bring her another.

"What do you want me to say?"

"Sometimes I really hate your psych degree." She muttered.

"I didn't say anything." I shrugged.

"You're judging me."

"I am not." But I kind of was.

"I can see you want to say something."

"Just be careful." I advised.

"What's that supposed to mean?" The waitress dropped offer another round for us; my second, her fourth.

"All I'm saying is be careful. This is the same man who hasn't exactly been honest and straightforward with you since day one." I reminded her.

"He was scared it would frighten me off." She made another excuse for the human excrement she was dating.

"You meet him, he tells you he's divorced and has a six-year-old son. Two weeks later, he says he has another ex-wife and a 21-year-old daughter plus a 19-year-old daughter." Shelly tried to interrupt me, but I continued. "And if that wasn't bad enough, you find out a month after that, that he has a three-year-old son and an eight-year-old daughter from yet another ex-wife — one that he spent two years in jail with for kidnapping. Each of these ex-wives left him for adultery and if my math is correct, having a six-year-old in the middle of this eight and three-year-old's, should tell you he's not known to be the faithful sort." I reasoned.

"He's made some mistakes." She took a long drink of her martini. "Brendon is nothing like that now."

"I'm just saying, be careful."

"He loves me." She said flatly.

"He's living with you, isn't he?" I already knew he was.

"I asked him to stay with me while he's building his new business." She explained.

"With your money."

"Haven't you ever helped someone? Given them a second chance?"

"Yes, but you are going into this blind. You only know what he tells you. Have you checked into his arrest?" I asked.

"No. I believe him."

"Well, just be careful is all I'm saying." Shelly knew how much I didn't like or trust the man. He had too many secrets, and his stories didn't add up.

"I love you for looking out for me, but Brendon is a good man who made a couple mistakes with the wrong women. And they were psycho bitches. Hell, look at my ex. I had no idea what he was doing until he was arrested. I got completely blindsided, and none of it made sense, even after he committed suicide in jail." Her voice dropped to a whisper.

"Please be careful." I reached across the table and laid my hand over hers.

"I trust him. He loves me." She assured me.

"Well, I've got to get going. I've got a presentation to work on for tomorrow." I reached for my purse.

"It's on me. You get the next one." She smiled.

"Deal." I stood up. "Are you okay to drive?"

"The office is one block over. I walked." She laughed a little.

"Good girl." I smirked. "I'll see you on Sunday. 5 a.m.?"

"Yep." She laid her debit card on the table. "I'll see you there. And remember, Arya. Love is a good thing."

"If you say so." I shook my head and walked towards the door.

~

Highway 10 was backed up across the city. I hated rush-hour traffic and had very little patience for it. I had hoped that it wouldn't be so bad just yet considering it was not quite three in the afternoon, but I was wrong.

But it gave me time to think. Here was a woman who was beautiful, tall, blonde; with a strong business sense but no common sense whatsoever. Her business was successful, but I had warned her that employing her son Garrett, who was merely days older than my own son and putting him in charge was not the smartest business decision. Garrett didn't have the maturity to lead the team that he was responsible for, and it was the only thing we disagreed on when I completed my assessment of her company.

Still, I had never seen a woman so unsure of herself and so desperate for love that she would allow any man into her life and into her bed that showed her any attention. I tried to warn her against it, but she was convinced that Brendon was a good man.

The stories he had told her about his past did not add up. When she had met him, he was living on the couch of some friends of his and had just been released from prison. She had met him on Match and immediately jumped into a bed with him. For months she had carried on a fling with both him and Matt.

She told me she couldn't make up her mind which one of them she wanted to be with. She still loved Matt despite his cheating ways. But in the end, she had chosen to be with Brendon despite his flaws and the mystery behind his past.

I wanted her to consider at least digging into his past. I felt that if she could at least get ahold of his arrest record, it would give her some information regarding the kidnapping. He had told her that his ex-wife had shown up to his work and was making a scene. After asking her to step into his office, she refused. So, he picked her up and carried her into his office to stop everyone from overhearing his personal business. He claims that because he forcibly moved her, he was charged with kidnapping.

The story didn't make sense to me. The fact that he received a couple years in jail for it made even less sense. Now she had moved this man into her home and wanted to build a life with him, as well as a business. I knew she could barely afford to give him the money that she was talking about, and it was the money that she had put back for her business to get off the ground. I warned her about taking risks, and money management was something she didn't understand well.

Shelly's desperate need for love and attention baffled me. I knew many women like her; insecure and unsure of themselves. They desperately wanted to be loved, and the last thing I wanted was to be like one of those women.

After the horrible divorce that I had experienced, I doubted that there was a man out there that could turn things around and make me fall in love with him. My best friend from home assured me that this man existed; that he was out there somewhere, and I would find him someday. I told her I was positive that my soul mate, my true love, the one man who was meant for me, had been hit by a bus when he was a small child.

After such a long and drawn out divorce, the only thing I could think of was focusing on my career. It had taken me so long to get where I am now and to think that someone could come along and destroy my life the way my ex-husband had was something I would never allow again. I couldn't believe that I had spent almost my entire adult life with someone who was so narcissistic, cruel, and downright mean. The damage he had done not only to myself but to my children was something that I just could never rationalize.

THREE

I CAME HOME FROM WORK on Friday from my last business meeting and started a fresh pot of coffee. I sat down at my desk and started going through the piles of paper on the new company I had just signed a contract with. They were trying to look for new ways to expand and stay competitive in an overly saturated design market.

I pulled out my laptop and started going through my emails. In the middle of all the business messages, there was one message from someone named Deuce that was sent from Match to my email as well as my phone. Out of curiosity, I opened it and began reading. He had responded to each little silly statement and sarcastic quip that I had put on my profile. Intrigued by his quick-witted comical replies, I opened his profile and began browsing.

It stated that he was 5 foot 10 inches, brown hair, blue eyes, and had at least one child still living at home. I pursued his pictures and had to admit he was very cute. I went back to my messages and decided what the hell, I'll go ahead and respond. I typed up a silly little nonsense response and sent it his way to see if he would reply.

I answered several more emails before I climbed out of my work clothes and jumped in the shower. It had been a long week, and the last thing I wanted to do was more work, but I also didn't feel like cooking dinner. I figured I would wait for Brylee to get home and then we could grab some dinner out.

After my shower toweled off and climbed into my silk robe. I poured myself a glass of white wine and went out on the balcony to enjoy the sunset. The sky was filled with hues of gold, amber, and purple as the desert sun faded behind the South mountain.

I sat down at my little Bistro table and began browsing through Facebook to see what my friends and family back in the Midwest were up to. The air was stifling hot as the desert heat baked early in June. I was already missing the cool days of spring and dreading the hot summer months still ahead.

A notification came up on my phone, letting me know that Deuce had replied. He sent back a charming little hello and wished me a happy Friday and asked if I had any special plans for the weekend. I typed back that I didn't other than working and playing golf on Sunday morning. He immediately responded that he was working on home renovations and that he had just finished the drywall and was getting ready to paint.

We spent the next hour and a half messaging cute little notes back and forth. I hated to admit how charming and witty he was. I enjoyed our humorous banter as he complained about having to do so much work to get his house back on the market as he wanted to move sometime soon.

Deuce asked me about my children and about what I did for a living. I briefly gave him minimal information as possible. He told me he had a 9-year-old daughter and had been divorced for 7 years. When I asked him about his career, he told me he was a police officer. As much as I enjoyed talking to him, I immediately put him in the *friend zone*.

Deuce was very charismatic, and in another life, I would have found him very attractive. But at this stage in my life having grown children of my own and a grandchild, I wasn't interested in dating someone with a minor child. I'd raised my children. I was done. I enjoyed my freedom, and I loved being able to come and go as I please. The last thing I wanted was to have to deal with babysitters again and even worse, the ex-wife. Not to mention that I still felt the same way about dating an officer.

However, there was something about Deuce that made him different. He had none of the arrogance Dylan had, nor did he constantly try to impress me. We had so much in common, and despite the obvious reasons I didn't want to date him, I truly enjoyed our conversations.

~

Brylee came home from work about seven, and we headed off to a steakhouse not far from our place. She was working part-time at a daycare center while going to school and was telling me it was the best form of birth control she could have ever imagined. She was working towards her degree in elementary education, specializing in children with special needs. But one particular child in her class, a 4-year-old little hellion, was driving her batty lately and she was about ready start looking for a new job.

She rambled throughout our dinner about work and school. She was a vibrant and energetic young lady, and I envied her youth. She had blossomed into a beautiful young lady since our move to Arizona, and the shy girl we'd left behind in Indiana had faded into darkness.

I was so proud of the woman she was growing into. She worked hard and was committed to her education, earning top grades. She pushed herself harder than anyone I knew.

Brylee flipped her long chestnut hair over her shoulder and

took another sip of her Sangria. She giggled with all the vitality of youth and innocence. She was a great kid with a huge heart.

"Are you going to see that officer again?" She asked, picking at her roll.

"No. I don't see the point."

"Momma, you're gonna have to give someone a chance."

"Darling, he wasn't the right one for me." I smiled. "If it makes you feel any better, I have been talking with someone. Sending messages really. Nothing much. But he's really funny and makes me laugh."

"That's great. Are you going to meet him?" She popped another piece in her mouth.

"I might, but he's no one I could ever date." I tilted my head and looked down at the table a bit disappointed in that reality.

"Why?"

"Because he's a cop for one and I won't date a cop. I don't want to be worrying every day when he goes off to work. You're forgetting, I was a military wife. I remember what it was like when your dad deployed and that constant worrying. I hated it. Besides, he has a nine-year-old daughter." I snorted. "I've raised my kids."

"But if you like him," Brylee started.

"Yes, I do. But only as a friend. He's someone I enjoy talking with. We have a lot in common."

"Perhaps you should try going out with him once before you stick him in the friend zone." She shook her head at me.

"What would be the point?" I shook my head back at her.

"He makes you laugh. You may have a really good time." She laughed a bit at me.

"Even if I did, it would be as friends only. He's not my type." I told her.

"Why is he "not your type."" Brylee raised her eyebrows at me.

"Here." I pulled up his Match profile and handed her my phone.

"He's cute." She said as she continued looking through his information.

"Unfortunately." I snorted. He was really cute.

"Okay, yeah. He's not like the men you're usually attracted to, but that could be a good thing." She reasoned and handed my phone back.

"You are impossible." I smirked and dropped my phone into my purse.

"Is he still texting you?"

"Yes."

"Have you spoken to him yet?"

"No. Just texting."

"I think you should meet him; have dinner. At least give him a chance, Momma, before you run the other way."

"I don't run." I rolled my eyes at her.

"Sprint more like it." She laughed.

"Are you done?"

"No, but I'll let it go for now." She gave me a cocky smile.

"How sweet of you." The child was definitely mine.

FOUR

THE NEXT MORNING, I WOKE before dawn and started the coffee. With my first cup of coffee in hand, I sat out on the balcony and watched the sunrise. It had been a long week, and I was exhausted.

The sun rising over the eastern mountains lit the sky into a matrix of golds, purples, and pinks. I checked my phone hoping I had another message from Deuce. He must have gotten up early to get some work done on his house. He told me he was having his morning coffee and waiting for Lowe's to open to go get some more paint. I messaged back good morning and told him to have a wonderful day.

Sunday morning, I met Shelly out at Ocotillo Golf Club and Resort in Chandler; the sight of my first date with Dylan. I had told Shelly how beautiful the course was, and she had decided we had to try it out.

We took the golf cart out to the first hole; thankfully, we weren't paired with anyone else. The ground was saturated to the point that we were squishing our way to tee-off.

"This is ridiculous." Shelly complained.

"How are we supposed to tee off in this?" I remarked, trying to get my tee to balance straight in the green.

"Next time we'll know to tee off a couple hours later after the grounds had a chance to absorb this. Hopefully, it will be better by the time we get to the fourth hole." She shrugged and continued stretching with the golf club.

"I hope so." I remarked and hit the worse drive of my life.

Shelly started laughing until hers disappeared into the lake off to the left side of the fairway.

"It's not so funny, is it?"

I loved our Sunday mornings on the course. Every Sunday, we tried a different course around Phoenix. It was such a wonderful and relaxing way to kick off the week. We drank our mimosas, drove the cart around like idiots, and laughed our way through eighteen holes. Thankfully, neither of us cared about how we did; although we were fiercely competitive with each other. It was all in good fun and necessary stress relief from the corporate world we were constantly engulfed in.

By the fifth hole, I confessed about Deuce.

"Deuce?" She wrinkled her forehead. "Does his mother not like him?"

"It's a nickname. I have no clue where it came from, but he's had it for years. He told me most people don't even know this real name." I chuckled.

"What's his real name?"

"Grayson, something German I can't pronounce." I shrugged. "It starts with an S."

"And you've already stuck him in the friend zone without ever meeting him?" She shook her head at me before she hit the ball off the fairway.

"Don't judge me. I've raised my kids. I finally made it out the other side of the tunnel." I climbed back into the cart. "I'm 45 years old."

"You don't ever think about having another one?" She climbed in beside me.

"Are you high?" I looked at her like she was crazy.

"Why not? You're still young enough."

"My baby will be 23 this fall." I stopped the cart between our two balls. "I can't even fathom starting all over again."

"I would if I could." She stated before getting out of the cart.

"Are you serious?" I stared at her as if she'd lost her mind.

"I love kids. I wish I'd had a dozen." She grinned and walked over to her ball.

"Yeah, says the woman who only has one." I snickered and rolled my eyes.

"But the idea of starting over with a nine-year-old — they are already set in their ways. Plus, you have to deal with the ex." I shook my head as we climbed back into the cart after we'd hit the ball.

"She may be a great kid." Shelly shrugged. "At least give him a chance before you stick him in the friend zone."

"I don't think so." I scowled at her.

"He may be worth it." She grinned.

"Yeah, because so many men are." I rolled my eyes again.

Over the next several holes, I let her read through his profile and all the messages we'd been sending back and forth. Then, Shelly spent the remainder of the course teasing me relentlessly about how cute we were with the silly and sarcastic messages Deuce and I continued exchanging throughout the morning. He was trying to talk me into going to dinner with him this evening, but I was very reluctant despite my daughters and Shelly's urging for me to take the chance. Deuce had a certain charm about him that was intoxicating. He was sweet and cute, and it seemed that everything he said made me laugh.

Deuce's persistence finally paid off by the time Shelly and I reached the seventeenth hole. I finally relented; agreeing to meet him for dinner that evening. I wasn't sure it was a good idea, but I had to admit to was extremely curious about this man. He seemed too good to be true. And when that happens, it always is.

By noon the sun was blazing overhead, and the temperature had reached the triple digits. Shelly and I walked back to our cars drenched in sweat. I couldn't wait to get home and lounge in the pool. I had agreed to meet Deuce at a Mexican restaurant at six.

~

I slipped into my bikini and decided I was going to lounge by the pool for a few hours when my phone dinged. I was eagerly waiting for another message from Deuce but instead saw I had a message from Dylan. He said he was on my side town, right around the corner from my place and wanted to know if I wanted to have lunch.

As I was reading Dylan's text, the message I'd been waiting for from Deuce finally arrived. I rested back on the raft in the pool and messaged him back. I didn't respond to Dylan. I didn't want to see him, and I wasn't sure how to tell him.

By three, I went back inside. I messaged Deuce back and told him I was looking forward to seeing him at six. I jumped into the shower, and I contemplated what I was going to wear. I wanted to look casual but nice. Unfortunately, most of my wardrobe was business attire. I had a few sundresses but couldn't decide on which one was appropriate.

My phone rang at half past four, and I jump to grab it while doing my makeup. It was Dylan. I stared at the phone, debating whether I was going to answer it and decided I couldn't be that cruel.

"Hi, Arya. How are you doing?" Dylan's voice was light and cheery.

"Good. How is your day going?"

"I called you because I was over by Target and thought I would stop in and see you and see if you wanted to have lunch."

"I'm sorry. I was out at the pool relaxing and trying to get a little bit of sun. I didn't have my phone with me." I lied. Usually, I didn't because of the heat, but today I took it just so I could continue talking to Deuce. "Are you still over here?"

"No. I'm sorry I'm back home. I guess we'll have to see if we can get together some other time. Did you golf this morning?" He asked.

"Yes, we went to the course where we were at."

"How did you do? Did you remember what I taught you?"

"I did. Thank you. It helped a lot."

"How many balls did you lose? He chuckled.

"More than I care to admit." I confessed.

"That many, huh?"

"Let's just say I'll be stopping by Golf Emporium before next Sunday."

"I warned ya." He continued taunting me.

"I know. That's why I brought an extra box with me."

"Well, I've got to get back to work. I'm staining the deck. I'll call ya this week and see if we can match up our schedules."

"Sounds good. Have a great afternoon, and don't work too hard."

I tossed my phone back on my bed and walked into my closet. I still had no idea what I was going to wear tonight. My makeup and hair were done. I had left it down, cascading over my shoulders in a blonde crown. My skin was bronzed and lotioned. I tried on several dresses and quickly discarded them, tossing them across my bed.

I tried on the fifth dress and turned around in the mirror when I heard Brylee giggle from the doorway.

"Nervous?"

"Shut up."

She came over and sat down on the corner of my bed.

"You look beautiful, momma." I smiled over at her. "Just remember to not fidget or ramble." She chuckled.

"Thanks." I smirked.

I finally settled on a cornflower blue sundress with a white trim that showed just enough cleavage to be suggestive but not provocative. It rested about four inches above my knees and showed off my shapely tanned legs. I slipped into my white sexy high-heel sandals. They completed the ensemble perfectly.

I spun around to face my daughter.

"What do you think?" I playfully posed for her.

"He's not going to know what hit him." She laughed.

~

I turned the radio up and headed toward Abuelo's Mexican restaurant. I hadn't even made it two miles from my home when my phone rang.

"Hello." I hit the button on my steering wheel, connecting me to my phone.

"Arya? This is Grayson. I'm having trouble finding the restaurant. I'm over at the Chandler Fashion Mall. I'm driving around the parking lot, and I don't see it." His sultry voice filled my car.

"What are you doing at the Chandler Mall? The restaurant is across the street from the mall." I rolled my eyes, tapping my steering wheel.

"You said it was at the mall." He sighed heavily.

"No. I said it was by the Chandler mall. Not at the Chandler mall." I laughed. "Aren't you a police officer? Shouldn't you know where the restaurant is?" I teased.

"I'm a Phoenix police officer, not a Chandler one. I don't know this area." I could hear the smile in his voice.

"Okay, if that's your excuse." It was fun tormenting him.

"It's not an excuse. It's the truth."

"But didn't you say you've lived here for twenty years?"

"Not in Chandler. I live in Mesa." He explained.

I was coasting down Chandler Boulevard when a barrage of red and blue lights cluttered my vision and blocked my path.

"Wonderful. I guess I'm going to be late. Your buddies have the road blocked up ahead and are rerouting traffic."

"They aren't my buddies."

"Well, they are being a pain in the ass, and I can't get through." I scoffed.

"Then go around; jump over to Ray Road and come up."

"Damn it! Move your ass!" I casually yelled at the driver in front of me. "I swear. People have no clue how to freakin drive down here."

"Oh, my gawd." Grayson laughed. "You're as bad as me."

"Idiot. Move!" I barely heard his continual laughter. "Jesus Christ." I exhaled loudly in exasperation.

"You kill me." I heard him mutter through my speakers.

"What?" Then I rolled my eyes at myself feeling foolish. "Sorry. It's a bad habit. I am an impatient driver, and I hate stupidity."

"So, you normally cuss people out while you drive?"

"Sorry." I confessed. "My friend, Daryl, in Indy swears I have Tourette's Syndrome because I'll be in the middle of talking about something and then just break into a barrage of profanity for a few minutes and then go right back to what I was talking about."

"My daughter yells at me all the time about it from the back seat. She's always going; 'Daddy, language' or at least she did when she was little. Lately, she's been yelling at drivers right along with me — but without the profanity of course."

I pulled into the parking lot and found a spot near the back. I shut off my car and took a silent deep breath.

"I'm here." I announced.

"Well, come on it." His voice was light and chipper.

"Okay."

FIVE

I CLOSED MY EYES, TOOK another deep breath, and got out of the car. I still didn't think this was a good idea. I really enjoyed the banter I shared with Deuce, and I didn't want to ruin our friendship by letting him think this was a date. I knew nothing could ever happen between us because of his profession and his daughter. It was simply something I didn't want in my life. The headache and the trouble both would bring wasn't what I wanted now that I finally had control of my life for the first time in almost twenty years.

Deuce was waiting for me just inside the door. He was every bit as striking in person as he was in his picture. He was dressed in a blue polo and jeans. He looked nice in a casual way and had an air of confidence about him that didn't have a shred of the arrogance Dylan displayed.

He stood almost six feet tall with broad shoulders, dark hair that was cut short and peppered with gray. He had piercing blue eyes the color of the sky on a spring morning. His arms were muscular and his chest broad, but clearly not as chiseled as he must have been a decade ago before he took a desk job.

"I put our name down for a table." Deuce smiled warmly as I approached. "You look nice."

"Thank you. So, do you." I couldn't help but smile back at him. I felt completely at ease in his presence.

The hostess called his name, and we followed her across the restaurant towards a booth in the back. I was pleased to see that he was still several inches taller than me despite my three-inch heels. I slid into the bench across from Deuce. The waitress pounced before we even picked up our menus.

"Hello, my name is Jasmine, and I'll be taking care of you tonight. Can I start you off with something to drink?" She smiled widely at Deuce.

"I'll have a Miller on tap if you have it," Deuce said politely.

"I'll take an iced tea, please."

"Right away." Jasmine smiled and scurried away.

"I'm glad you decided to come." His smile was comforting.

"Me too."

"So, what made you move to Arizona?" He rested his elbows on the table and fidgeted with his fingers. It was nice to see he was just as nervous as I was.

"Divorce. You?"

"My parents moved down here when I was in the military with my younger brother. I really didn't have any reason to go back to Pennsylvania after I got out. So, I moved here." He rambled. "I got a job moving furniture right after the service and then joined the department. I've been there for the last eighteen years. I moved over to homicide about ten years ago, I guess. I started in night detectives, and now I'm in the violent crimes unit."

"So, you're an actual homicide detective?" He nodded. "I'm sure you stay busy down here." I smirked.

"Very." He shrugged with a grin. "It goes in spurts."

"And you've been divorced for seven years?"

"Yes."

"You only have the one child?"

"That's right. Madelyn. Maddie." He smiled. "She's nine. And you have two?"

"A boy and a girl. My son, Carson, is married and in the military. He's has a little boy that will be a year old in August. My daughter, Brylee, lives with me. She works part-time as a preschool teacher and goes to ASU."

"I started a little late." Deuce chuckled.

"I guess I started a bit early. I was nineteen when my son was born." I shrugged. "Does your daughter live with you?"

"Mostly. I have her Friday through Tuesday."

"Seriously?" He nodded. "Where is she tonight?"

"She went with her mom to visit her grandparents in Wisconsin. She'll be home on Saturday."

"So, you have her every weekend?"

Good Lord, this was never going to work.

"Pretty much. But my parents got divorced last year, and my mom moved in with me. She helps me with running her to school or picking her up or if I want to go somewhere."

"You live with your mom?"

Unbelievable!

"No. My mom moved into my house." He explained — it still didn't sound any better his way; he still lived in the same house with his mother!

"It's good she's there to help you out." It took every ounce of my willpower not to walk out of the restaurant.

"The hours I work and being on call every four days, it's been a blessing to have her help."

"Doesn't her mom ever take care of her?"

"No. My ex, Cathy, likes the idea of Madelyn, but not the actual job of taking care of her or being a mom. She's the same way with her son, Caleb from her first marriage. He lives with his dad and only sees her a couple days a month."

"If you know she was a shitty mom, why did you ever marry her; let alone have children with her?" I couldn't help but ask.

"I was lonely and wanted to get married." He answered, honestly. "I thought she would change, but she never did. She got worse. She was diagnosed as bipolar with a borderline personality disorder."

"She must be a delight."

What a freaking train wreck —Run!

"She is."

Deuce spent the next hour telling me all about his psychotic ex-wife and all I could think about was sprinting to the door. He was a great storyteller, and his spin on her erratic behavior was humorous. I was surprised he still held onto an ounce of his sanity considering the hell this certifiable lunatic had put him through during their marriage and still inflicts on him by using their daughter as a pawn in her petty torments.

I told him about my children and the joys of my divorce over dessert. After hearing about his experiences, mine didn't even come close despite the hell my ex, Todd, had put me through. From everything he was telling me, I truly hoped she was on medication.

"Okay. I have to ask the million-dollar question." I couldn't stop myself from asking. "How long have you been on Match?"

"I joined in February. I'd tried it before. That's how I met Amber." He shrugged. "After we broke up, I thought I'd give it a shot. What about you?"

"I got railroaded into it. My friend, Shelly, joined last fall and was constantly making me browse through profiles for her. I finally relented and got a six-month subscription." I explained.

"And have you had any luck?" He asked.

"One really great first date, but a horrible second date. And then a few worse first dates that never deserved a second." I couldn't help but laugh. "What about you?"

"I've gone out on several dates with a few different women, but I haven't met anyone that I'd consider a relationship with." I gave him points for honesty.

"Okay, I have a confession to make." I debated for a moment and decided to come clean. "Do you know a Lieutenant Dylan Wagner?"

"Yeah, I know Dylan. Why?" Deuce folded his arms and looked at me curiously.

"I met him on Match." Deuce started laughing.

"Seriously?"

"Yes. And I went on a date with him last weekend."

"No second date?"

"He's called several times and texted. He offered to take me to lunch, but I made up some excuse." I said truthfully.

"Why is that, can I ask?"

"Honestly?" I was hesitant to tell him.

"Yes. I'm curious." A devious smile spread across his shapely lips.

"He's a bit too arrogant for me." Deuce laughed wholeheartedly. "All he did was talk about himself. He bragged about his work with the Special Olympics and said he used to live in California and worked as a model."

"Oh, my God!" He laughed even harder. "That doesn't surprise me at all. Did he tell you about his appearance on the show *Family Matters*? Or his time as a Chip N' Dale dancer?"

"No, but that doesn't surprise me at all. He did show me an old modeling picture of himself."

"Priceless." He shook his head, still laughing. "He honestly believes women are impressed that he did that shit twenty years ago. Badge bunnies, perhaps, but no respectable woman."

"Badge bunnies?"

"Women who specifically date cops." Deuce explained.

"Seriously? And here I've been avoiding it for thirty years." I grinned. "And now have managed two dates in less than two weeks. That's terrible. But in my defense, I didn't know he was a cop."

"So, his charming arrogance didn't impress you?"

"About as much as the gym picture he sent me." I picked up my phone and pulled up Dylan's text messages. I scrolled down to the picture he'd sent me and handed the phone to Deuce.

"Good grief." He laughed and handed my phone back. "And you weren't dazzled by that?"

"Hardly." I giggled. "And another slight issue of his I guess you could say I wasn't too impressed by."

"Huh?" He looked confused.

"Let's just say I wasn't overly impressed when he was correcting my golf swing." Deuce wrinkled his forehead. "When he was standing behind me, pressed up against me." I held up my pinky finger and laughed.

"Don't tell me that!" He spat laughing. "I don't want to know that! I have to work with the guy. I do see him on occasion."

"Sorry. It was just too funny. I had to tell you." Tears of laughter leaked from the corner of my eyes, and I wiped them away with my napkin.

"You realize now every time I see him, that's going to enter my mind!"

"I'm sorry. I couldn't help it." I tried to explain.

"I guess that explains why his wife left him for a woman." His face was red from laughing so hard.

"My friend, Shelly, and I have nicknamed him..."Needles." See," I showed him my phone again. "That's what he's listed under."

"He would die if he knew that."

"How could he not know? I mean, there are locker rooms. He

would have to have noticed the deficiency." I reasoned trying to control my giggles.

"Men don't look."

"That's good to know. But you would think they would still know, at least what's the average size I would think."

"I suppose." He tried to shrug casually, but his own laughter was fighting through. "I've never had any complaints."

"Good to know." I playfully rolled my eyes at him with a mischievous smirk.

We finally made it out to the parking lot where we stood next to my car for another hour talking about anything and everything. I couldn't recall the last time I'd enjoyed someone's company so much. He had the best sense of humor. He was witty, sarcastic, and could take as much as he dished out.

"Well, I'd better get going." I said for the third time. "I have an early meeting tomorrow morning. Don't you have to get up early?"

"No. I'm off on Monday's."

"Must be nice." I teased.

"I would like to see you again." He said sheepishly. I loved how he could look so boyish one moment and a sexy detective the next.

"I'd like that."

"I'll talk to you tomorrow." Deuce stood there, awkwardly.

"I look forward to it." I leaned over and gave him a quick hug. It was almost painful, and by his nonreceptive reaction, I wasn't sure whether he was happy I did it or not.

Embarrassed, I climbed into my car and headed home. I felt I'd made a stupid mistake. Clearly, Deuce had decided to also place me in the friend zone, and I was too stupid to see it. I felt like an idiot.

I crawled into bed and pulled the covers up to my chin. I closed my eyes and kept seeing Deuce's face when I hugged him.

He almost looked mortified. I couldn't shake the disappointing feeling in my chest.

I had decided to put him in the friend zone, but after our dinner, I wasn't sure that's where I really wanted him. I felt so confused and hurt. I really enjoyed our time together. We had so much in common, liked the same things, held the same morals. Plus, we were both sarcastic smart-asses who loved to pick on each other relentlessly.

I was regretting my quick judgment to put him in the friend zone and was now hurt that he'd placed me there as well.

I was starting to drift off to sleep when my phone rang. I reached over to the empty pillow beside me and grabbed it without looking.

"Hello."

"Hi." The sound of Deuce's voice made my heart leap.

"I was just thinking about you." I confessed.

"I was thinking about you too. I had a really good time tonight." His voice was soft and smooth.

"I did too." I paused, not sure I should ask what I was dying to know. "So, you weren't disappointed?"

"Disappointed? Why would I be disappointed?"

"In me." I didn't want to tell him how badly my ex had damaged my self-esteem.

"Why would I be disappointed in you?" He chuckled a bit.

"I don't know. Maybe I wasn't what you were expecting." I sounded foolish to my own ears.

"You are amazing. You're beautiful, sexy, smart. You're more than I expected."

"You're sweet." I rested back on the pillow and closed my eyes. Images of his crystal blue eyes, boyish smile, and easy laugh flooded my brain.

"So, you weren't disappointed?"

"Not at all. You make me laugh. You're charming. And those

blue eyes ..." I paused for a moment. "talk about sexy." I said in a sultry voice.

"Agh." He sighed heavily. "I've heard crap about my eyes all my life."

"I can see why. They are stunning."

"Thanks," he said shyly.

"Are you already in bed?"

"Yes."

"Me too."

"So, what made you decide to be a business psychologist?" He asked.

"Business psychologist?" I smiled to myself. "I'm an industrial-organizational psychologist or I/O psychologist in private practice. I analyze the market and assist organizations in restructuring or redesigning in order to be successful in growing economic markets" I explained.

"I got bored with college after a semester. I ended up leaving and joining the Marines."

"I didn't go back to college until my early thirties. It wasn't easy with a family, but I loved college. I love new challenges and learning new things." I confessed.

"I didn't fit in at school, high school, or college. But when I joined the Marines, I found my place."

"So, why didn't you re-up?"

"After two deployments and getting to live in Hawaii, Singapore, Hong Kong, Kuwait, Jordan, Africa, and several others, I was tired of being deployed. Out of the three and a half years I was stationed in Hawaii, I only spent maybe ten months on the island."

"That sounds fun, though; getting to see the world."

"Not as much as you think. The traveling got old. I wanted to stay in one place long enough to make it a home."

"What was your MOS?" I asked.

"I was a military analyst."

"That sounds interesting."

"It was great when I was in my twenties. I can't imagine living that lifestyle now." He chuckled.

"True. It wouldn't work well with having a family. But many people do it."

"I wouldn't want to."

"It's difficult. I hated it when I was a Marine wife, and I see how difficult it is on my daughter-in-law. But she handles it much better than I did."

"That's good. I feel like my work keeps me away from my daughter too much as it is. I miss a lot with her, and I hate it. I wouldn't be able to work the hours demanded of me without my parents' help." He confessed.

"I still can't believe Cathy has no interest in her daughter. My kids are everything to me."

"You're also not mentally ill."

"True."

"Her suicide attempts, her mental illnesses, her manipulation of me, her domineering parents; all add up to one heartless shrew who only thinks of herself without consideration of how her actions affect her daughter's mental stability." His words sounded heated but also hurt.

"My ex is a manipulative bastard that's done everything to destroy me and damage my relationship with my children. Thankfully, they saw right through him. Brylee never believed his lies, but it took Carson a while. Things are still not back to normal between us. Hopefully, they will be once again. But he said some horrible things to me after I left and even though we're speaking again, it's hard to forget." I confessed. "I've done everything for my children. I'm not perfect, and I've made mistakes as a parent."

"We all have Arya." Deuce reassured me.

"Still, his words cut deep through my heart. His wife, Alicia, told me he was in a dark place after he got back from his second deployment and took his anger out on everyone, but because he and I have always been so close, I was his perfect target."

"Does he have PTSD?"

"Yes, I believe so."

"Then you know it has nothing to do with you." His voice was tender and loving.

"The clinical side of me knows that, but as a mother, it broke my heart." I explained.

"I understand." He whispered. "But you know the nature of that beast. It's surrounded by darkness and intense sadness."

"I know." His compassion astounded me.

We spent the next four hours talking about everything. He told me more about his childhood in Pennsylvania and Maryland, pets he had, the sports he played. He was so endearing and charming. I couldn't remember the last time I had enjoyed talking to someone.

When I finally drifted off to sleep, my thoughts were filled with him.

SIX

I COULDN'T GET DEUCE OUT of my mind from the moment I woke up until my meeting started. I focused my attention long enough to go through my proposal, smile and shake hands, and assure the new CEO that we would do everything possible to make the transition period as smooth as possible during the reorganization.

It was almost two o'clock before I headed home. I checked my phone for the millionth time — no message from Deuce. Only two texts from Dylan and additional emails needing my attention. I discarded Dylan's messages. He held no interest to me.

By three, Deuce finally messaged me asking me how my meeting went. I quickly sent him a message back, telling him everything went fine. I hated to admit how thrilled and relieved I was just to receive a message from him.

Deuce responded back saying he'd been painting the living room all day. I was trying to get my little dog, DaVinci on his lease for a walk, but he has the tendency to go ballistic when I get home and wouldn't stand still. Rather than fight with him and try to text; I decided to just call him.

"Hey stranger, how are you?" Deuce picked up on the second ring.

"Sorry, I'm trying to walk DaVinci and I can't exactly text. It was easier to just call you." I immediately explained and then felt ridiculous for doing so.

"I understand. I have three dogs myself."

"That's a lot."

"Yeah well, it wasn't planned. My brother added to my collection." He laughed. "Oh well, the more, the merrier."

"I understand. I had three dogs when my children were growing up." I turned the corner and guided DaVinci across the street. "Did you have a good day?"

"Not really. I picked up the paint this morning, and some idiot stopped abruptly in front of me, I hit the breaks, and the paint fell off the passenger seat and went all over the floor and the door of my truck."

"Why in the world did you put paint on the seat?" I laughed.

"I don't know. I just did." I could hear the smile in his voice.

"Don't you know you're supposed to set it on the floor." I loved picking on him.

"Yeah, I figured that out."

"Don't you do anything for fun?" I inquired.

"What do you have in mind?"

"I don't know." I hadn't given it any thought. "Let's go somewhere out of the ordinary. Someplace different."

"Like where?"

"I don't know. You're the one who's been here twenty years. Don't you know of anything fun like a quirky ice cream shop or themed restaurant or something?" I asked.

"I'm sure there is, but none that I know of." Deuce admitted.

"Then I guess you had best start digging." I chuckled.

"And when are we going to this unusual place?"

"Tonight." I was having fun playing with him.

"Really? What time?"

"Six thirty."

"That doesn't give me much time." He complained.

"Then I suppose you'd better get busy on some research."

"I don't even have your address."

"Oh, you're picking me up?" I walked back up the driveway with DaVinci leading the way.

"Yes."

"I'll text it to you." I walked into the living room and hung DaVinci's lease on the hook. He headed straight to his water dish.

"Sounds good. I'll see you soon."

"I look forward to it." I walked into my room and tossed my cell on my bed. I was in dire need of a shower and had little time to come up with something to throw on.

I took a cold shower to combat the triple digits outside. I stood in front of the vanity in my silk robe with my hair in a towel. I had no clue what to put on because I had no idea where we were headed.

I settled on a white two-piece dressy short outfit with wide navy-blue strips. It was almost backless with only to straps that crossed across my back. The shorts were pleated and looked more like a mini skirt. It was one of my favorite outfits. I wore it with brick red sandals that wrapped around my legs just above the ankle and tied in the back.

I left my long blond hair down with loose big curls cascading across my shoulders and down my back. I kept my makeup light as it was early in the evening.

Deuce arrived on time and opened his truck door for me. I immediately noticed the splattered dark cornflower blue paint all over the passenger door and floorboard. I burst out laughing as he smirked and shut the door abruptly as I climbed into the seat.

"Shut up." He grinned, taking a seat on the driver's side.

"I'm sorry, but it's funny. I thought you said you'd cleaned it up." I said as we pulled out of my neighborhood.

"I did." He stated with a smile and rolled his eyes at me.

"If you say so." I muttered loud enough for him to hear me. I loved giving him as much grief as possible. I'm not even sure why, except that it was because he always dished it back at me.

"It's a truck." He shrugged but continued to grin.

"So, where are we going?" I was curious to see what he'd come up with.

"Do you like Italian? Pizza?"

"Of course."

"Good. I found this restaurant that makes these specialized deserts. I thought it would be fun to check it out."

"Sounds wonderful."

We made small talk about our day on our journey. He explained how much he hated remodeling and couldn't wait to sell his house. He'd bought it about eighteen years ago shortly after joining the department. He simply hated the memories it held from his ex-wife and all the antics she's pulled there. He admitted that he'd torn it down almost to the bones and was handling most of the remodeling himself with some assistance from his partner, Ernesto.

Deuce pulled into a strip mall parking lot and parked in front of the restaurant whose section of the lot was surprisingly vacant.

"Are they open?" I asked when he turned off the truck.

"They should be. It's Monday."

"Did you check when you looked it up?"

"No." He confessed but climbed out anyways. I followed.

We walked up to the front doors noticing all the lights were out, and it was empty. The sign on the door said they were closed on Mondays and Tuesdays. I snickered and touched the side of his arm.

"Now what?" I asked.

"It didn't even occur to me they'd be closed today." He looked embarrassed.

"Well, there's a candy store a couple doors down. Let's have a look." I offered, but he hesitated. "Oh, come on." I chuckled and tugged on his arm a bit to nudge him along.

The candy store was a Toys R Us of sweets. It was huge and had everything imaginable for the sweet tooth. There were singles and tubs and even things that I hadn't seen on the shelves in years since my childhood.

We walked up and down the aisles browsing through the various delights. There was such an array of sweets to give any dentist heart failure. I picked up Brylee's favorite candy, Now & Later's that was a little challenging at times to find. I also purchased a couple of caramel suckers for her and me to share as we did many times throughout her childhood.

"What would you like to do about dinner? Is there anything you are in the mood for?" He asked on our way back to his truck.

"Pizza still sounds good."

"All right. Let's see what's close-by." He pulled out his phone and started searching for pizza joints near where we were at. "There's one about a mile and a half from us."

"Okay." I climbed back up into the truck, and Deuce closed the door behind me.

The small restaurant was jammed full of people. The hostess informed us it would be about a fifteen-minute wait. So, we stood in a little spot by the front door almost pressed up against one another, which was most awkward, considering we had not yet kissed. And after his reaction the night before, I was beginning to wonder if we ever would despite our wonderful conversations.

Deuce reached for the check before I could and smiled sweetly.

"Please. Let me get this one. You paid for dinner last night." I playfully tried to take it from him, but he snatched it up quickly.

"Sorry. I can't. I've never been able to let a woman pay for dinner." He shrugged with a mischievous grin.

"You're a saint." I teased back. "You must not date a lot."

"I have my fair share." His coy smile was adorable. "Can we get a box, please?" He asked the waitress as she accepted the check.

"Well, thank you for dinner." I reached over and lightly touched his hand for a moment.

"You're welcome. I had a great time."

"Me too." The waitress came back and handed the little black book to Deuce and placed the box on the table.

He signed the slip, and I put all the leftovers in the box. I attempted to hand them to him as we walked out of the restaurant.

"No, please. Those are for you." He smiled. "Didn't you say that your daughter was home? Perhaps she'd like them."

"You did this for Brylee?" I nodded towards the box.

"She doesn't like leftovers?" He hesitated.

"Are you kidding?" He opened the door for me. "She's thrilled if she doesn't have to cook. She loves leftovers." I chuckled.

Deuce closed the door and went around and climbed in the driver's side. "I hope she likes Italian."

"She loves it. And it was very thoughtful of you to think of her." I smiled over at him. "Very sweet."

Deuce smiled uncomfortably and started the truck. "Hmm. Did you see the way that man looked at you while we were waiting to be seated?" He pulled out into traffic.

"What are you talking about? What man?"

"He was easily in his late fifties or early sixties. He was there with his wife and another couple. They were exiting and walked by us. His wife was right behind him." He was trying to control his laughter to tell the story. "Most men will check out a lady with only their eyes and give them the once over, up and down, without being too obvious. But this guy, he bobbed his entire head up and down checking you out and was so obvious about it. I was like 'damn dude, really!' If he hadn't been older, I would have said something because it was that disrespectful to you and to me, but his age is also what made it so funny."

"Oh, dear Lord. I didn't even see him."

"I'm surprised his wife didn't smack him, but she was completely oblivious." He continued laughing.

He continued teasing me the rest of the way to my place. He pulled up in front and sat there for a moment.

"I had a wonderful time tonight." I wasn't sure what to say.

"Next time, I promise I'll make sure the place is open before I try to take you somewhere." He opened his truck door and walked around to open mine.

"Thanks." I took his hand and climbed down. "Please give me a call when you get home, so I know you made it all right."

"You do realize that it's a ten-minute drive to my house from here." He rolled his eyes playfully at me but continued to smile.

"Just the same. I would appreciate it."

"Fine."

Despite my better judgment, I leaned up and wrapped my arms around his neck. I wasn't sure if he wanted me to or not since he had avoided touching me all evening. I hesitated a moment and kissed him briefly on the cheek before I let him go.

Deuce looked at me almost as if I'd kicked his puppy. Humiliated, I said a short thank you and quick goodbye before rushing to the confines of my home. I shut the door behind me and leaned against it. I closed my eyes and took a deep breath. I wanted to sink into the floor and disappear.

Why had I kissed him on the cheek?

I shook my head slowly feeling like the most unattractive woman on the face of the earth.

"I'm guessing your date didn't go well." Brylee was sitting on the family room couch and watching me.

"Unfortunately, it went too well." I dropped my things on the bar, walked over and plopped down beside her, and removed my sandals. I propped my legs across her lap and laid back against the cushions.

"What does that mean? I thought you said he wasn't your type and you didn't want to get involved with him." The skepticism was written across her face.

"I know. I know." I felt like I was close to tears. "He's not my type at all. He's the opposite of everyone I've ever had a date with since high school. But there's something about him." I let out a long sigh. "He makes me laugh, and he's kind. I can talk to him for hours about anything. I truly enjoy his company."

"I suspected as much." She smirked.

"What?"

"You like him."

"He's nice. And funny. That's all." I started to get up, but she grabbed my legs.

"Admit it." She teased.

"I admit nothing." I rolled my eyes and climbed off the couch. She didn't stop me but continued laughing at me until I shut my bedroom door behind me.

No sooner did I get into my pajamas did my phone ring. It was Deuce.

"I'm home. And in one piece." The smile returned to his voice.

"Good to know." I crawled beneath the duvet and flipped on the television but turned the volume down low enough so I could talk.

The casual phone call finally ended at two in the morning; five hours since I'd returned home from our date. I laid the cell phone on the pillow beside me and tried to rationalize his behavior.

Deuce loved to tease me, pick on me, and at times treated me like one of the guys. Other times he acted like he was interested in me as something more than a friend. But when I'd kissed him on the cheek, he didn't seem overly thrilled by it. Still, our conversations were never dull. We laughed a great deal and genuinely enjoyed one another's company.

Now, I was more confused than ever before. I had no idea where I stood with him.

SEVEN

THE NEXT MORNING, I PUSHED all thoughts of him out of my mind and got ready for work. I had a great deal to do for my new client and wanted to get there early before the employees showed up. They had several departments that were none too thrilled about the changes being made, which was expected, but if their resilience wasn't put in check, it could easily spread like wildfire throughout the organization.

I tore myself away just after three in the afternoon, exhausted from a long day's work. Traffic was already backed up as I slowly inched my way across Phoenix. Flustered and irritated, I decided I needed to hear a friendly voice. I called Deuce.

"Hello stranger, how was your day?" He sounded cheerful.

"Long. How was yours?"

"I'm still painting. I'm almost done."

"And then what will you do with the rest of your week?"

"Hopefully, get the living room cleared out and work on the patio. My mother moved in with me when I started this mess, and all her stuff is piled everywhere, making it impossible for me to get anything done."

Our conversation drifted to family and the relationship he had with his parents and brother, Greg. Greg had moved to South Carolina last year with his wife and stepson. It sounded like they used to be very close, but he had married a very difficult woman who had also been diagnosed as bipolar — I guess the brothers were a great deal alike. Deuce referred to her as 'Cathy-light.' He said she wasn't as bad as his ex but was a raging bitch none the less.

Our conversation ran through dinner, and I glanced at the clock once more. I had a lot of research to do before tomorrow, and I was already tired. I longed to take a hot shower and go to bed, but that wasn't going to happen anytime soon. However, I couldn't bring myself to end our conversation. I was genuinely enjoying myself.

I mentioned to Deuce several times that I needed to get some research done before tomorrow, and every time the subject shifted, and we would launch into another topic. I slowly watched the hours drift by, and still, I couldn't bring myself to end the conversation. I simply loved talking with him.

At nine o'clock, I had managed to open my laptop, pull up the pages I needed, and put the title on my report. I had begrudgingly accepted the fact that it was going to be a long night.

"Are you expecting anyone?" Brylee poked her head in my room.

"No. Why?"

"Someone just knocked on the door." I barely heard her over DaVinci's nervous breakdown.

"Are you going to let me in?" I barely registered Deuce's voice over the racket.

"What?"

"Are you going to let me in?" He repeated.

"Seriously? You're here?"

I scrambled off my bed and hurried past a confused Brylee. I didn't bother checking but flung open the front door. It was then that I realized I was wearing pajama shorts and a tank top.

"What are you doing here?" I blurted before I could stop myself.

"You said you had a ton of research to do tonight for your thing tomorrow." I stepped back and let him enter. "I figured I'd help since I've occupied your evening." His smile was infectious.

"You are amazing!" I couldn't stop smiling. I wanted to throw my arms around him, but I didn't dare. "This is my daughter, Brylee."

"Hi. Nice to meet you." Deuce greeted her.

"This is Grayson."

"So, you're the infamous Deuce I've been hearing about." Brylee walked over and stood beside me.

"I guess." He looked over at me and chuckled. "I've heard a lot about you too."

"All bad, I hope." A devious grin spread across her shapely lips.

"Not at all." He turned towards me. "I guess we'd better get to work." It was only then that I noticed he was carrying a briefcase. "I brought my laptop."

He was incredible.

I led him into my room and closed the door behind us. Deuce sat down in my desk chair and started setting up his computer on my desk. I climbed back up on my bed and put my laptop on my lap.

"I can't believe you're here." I couldn't stop smiling.

That was it, and I knew it. I was in love with him.

"I felt guilty." He shrugged with a grin.

"You are amazing." I stared at him.

"I think you are too." Our eyes met across the room and held each other for a moment. "Tell me what to do."

By midnight everything was completed, and it was better

than I ever anticipated. The charts and graphs were done, the statistics aligned, the report was finalized. I was so proud of the work we had done. I hit save and shut my laptop.

"Thank you so much. I couldn't have done this without you."

"Yes, you could have. I barely did anything." He got up and took a seat beside me on the bed.

"You did a lot." I whispered.

Our eyes met, and I was at a loss for words. I couldn't explain why I was so drawn to him. I felt a connection to him that I had never experienced before. He was so kind, considerate, and compassionate. He was genuine.

And I was head over heels in love with him.

"Can I kiss you?" Deuce's voice was barely above a whisper.

I could barely nod before he leaned over and brushed his lips lightly across mine.

My thighs went up in flames.

His hands slid around my back and drew me to him. I felt lightheaded, exhilarated.

He pressed his lips more firmly to mine. He tasted sweet, like the Swedish Fish he'd been snacking on. I felt his tongue brush lightly over mine.

I wrapped my arms around his neck and pressed his body against mine. I could feel his heart pounding in his chest. His hands gripped me firmly; rubbing over my skin intensely.

My hands slid up the back of his shirt. His skin was warm and soft. I pulled it up and over his head and discarded is carelessly. Deuce paused, looking at me with such longing.

"Are you sure?"

"Yes." I confessed.

I pulled him back to me and kissed him passionately. Clothes were discarded without haste. Deuce's hands grabbed, groped, fondled, massaged, teased, and tormented every inch of my body.

His lips tasted every particle of my skin. My body was on fire. I couldn't get enough of him.

I tugged on his hair as his lips worked their magic. My nails dug into his skin. I lightly bit at his shoulder, his chest. I wanted him. I pushed him over and straddled his thighs. I raked my nails over his chest and then leaned down, kissing him deeply; my tongue searching his mouth, absorbing him.

I pinched his nipples roughly and quickly discovered he loved it. I playfully bit at them, teasing them with my tongue. Deuce closed his eyes and groaned. He placed his hands on my shoulders and gently nudged me downward.

I gladly worked my way down, gliding my tongue over the happy trail that ran down his sculpted abdomen. His cock twitched and throbbed eagerly the closer I got to it. I could see the tip glistening with anticipation.

I wrapped my fingers around it squeezing it tightly in my hand and graciously slid down his thighs. I looked up into his crystal blue eyes and smiled deviously at him. He grinned back with a look of pure satisfaction on his face. I brought his cock to my mouth and lightly licked the top of it lavishing in the sweet taste of him.

The muscles in Deuce's body tightened, and he inhaled deeply. I took the head of it in my mouth and sucked on it like a lollypop. I loved the little noises he made as I guided it down my throat. His cock twitched and throbbed in my mouth. I moved slowly up and down his member while my hand massaged his testicles. I continued until his cock was a beautiful shade of purple, and I knew he was in agony.

I kissed my way back up his chest until my body was perfectly aligned with his. I kissed him deeply and put his cock inside me. I arched my back as I slid down his hard pole. He filled me gloriously. I loved the feel of him deep inside me. I rocked back and forth, gyrating my body over him. I held his biceps to balance myself. His pelvic bone grazed my clitoris, sending electric shocks through my body.

I threw my head back and rode him into ecstasy. He moaned loudly and tightened his hold on my hips, arching his back and thrusting his pelvic deep into me. His body shook and went rigid as he reached his climax.

I collapsed upon him. Our hearts were pounding harmoniously in our sweaty chests; labored breathing slowly returning to normal. I closed my eyes and breathed in the smell of his skin. I kissed the side of his neck.

"I'm so glad I answered your message."

"Me too." His voice was raspy.

I slid off to the side of him. My head was lying right above his heart. Its beat was steady and strong, lulling me off into a peaceful sense of security.

Deuce wrapped me tightly in the nook beneath his arm. I couldn't imagine being anywhere else. I was perfectly happy. I could not remember ever feeling this way with anyone in my life.

EIGHT

DEUCE WENT HOME LONG enough the next day to get a change of clothes. When he returned, I noticed he brought more than one change of clothes. I acted like I didn't notice, but I was thrilled.

Thursday night, I arrived home to find him waiting for me. He was sitting outside, waiting in his truck reading a book. He rolled down his window as I approached.

"I'm sorry, I'm late." I apologized.

"No problem. I understand." He turned off his truck and opened the door. He rolled up the window and stepped out.

"Have you been here long?" I asked as we walked up to my place.

"I was here on time." Deuce playfully nudged me.

"I'm twenty minutes late." I smirked. "I said I was sorry."

"Okay. Fine." I unlocked the door. "What would you like to do tonight?" He asked.

"What are you in the mood for?" I set my things down on the counter in the kitchen and went to retrieve DaVinci's leash.

"I'll take him out." He offered. "I know you hate walking him in heels." He smiled and walked out with DaVinci bouncing and barking at his heels.

I took off my dress and heels and put on my silk robe. I wasn't sure what he had in mind for the evening and didn't want to make any assumptions. Deuce was mischievous at times and loved to play his little games.

"I was thinking about going to the movies tonight. I've wanted to see *Deadpool* 2." He leaned on the doorframe of my bedroom.

"*Deadpool* 2?" He truly was a kid at heart.

"Have you seen the first one?" He came over and sat down in my desk chair.

"Yes. My daughter made me watch it."

"You didn't like it?" He put his feet up on the corner of my bed. I fought every urge in me to tell him to take his feet — his shoes, off my bed.

"It was funny." I vaguely recalled the film.

"It was hilarious." He said excitedly.

"I'm sorry. I haven't had time to see many movies or watch much television in the last several years." I preferred books over other mediums. "If I have a free moment, I read."

"I understand. But sometimes you have to relax." He tilted his head to one side with a grin.

"I do. Reading is relaxing to me."

"I get it. I love to read too. But you need to learn how to relax."

"I do relax." I argued.

"No. You occasionally sleep. If you are awake, you're working. I've never seen someone who works so much. You're constantly working on something. Even if we are in the car, you're on your phone looking something up — researching something or other." He chuckled slightly. "You never stop."

"I enjoy my job. What's so wrong with that?" I suddenly felt defensive.

"Nothing. But there is more to life than work."

"Not right now, there isn't. I'm sorry, but it's true." He couldn't possibly know how hard I worked to rebuild my life, my business, after my ex did all he could to destroy my world.

"You'll see." Deuce playfully rolled his eyes at me as his phone buzzed.

He glanced down at it and tapped the decline emblem before stuffing it back into his pocket.

"Who was that?" I asked.

"Amber." He shrugged casually.

"So, what time does the movie start?" I attempted to change the subject.

"6:10."

"Okay." I fumbled through my drawers and pulled out a pair of shorts.

"Want to get something to eat first? I'm starving."

"Sure." I pulled a shirt out of my closet and put it on. "But we should probably get tickets first."

"It's Thursday. We should be fine." He stood up and pushed the chair back under my desk.

"All right." I picked up my purse and followed him out.

We pulled into the parking lot a bit after six o'clock. We had dinner at Fried Pie and snuggled into the oversized recliners at the theatre to watch *Deadpool 2*.

I had a wonderful time. We walked hand in hand all evening and constantly teased and joked with each other. I felt as if I was walking in a cloud.

Deuce pulled into a little strip mall by my place on our way home. The air was sticky and humid. The desert stars were drowned out by the suburban lights. The shadow of south mountain loomed over the backdrop of the row of shops.

"How about some sundaes?" He took my hand as I climbed out of the truck.

"Are you trying to make me fat?" I teased. "We've been eating out a lot."

"You look perfect just the way you are."

"Wow. You really do need your eyes checked."

"My eyes are perfect." A smile spread across his face reaching his eyes and making them glisten in the lights.

"As is the rest of you." I laughed as he held open the door to Baskin Robbins.

"Hardly." He scoffed. "What do you think Brylee would like?" He scanned over the menu.

"You want to get Brylee some ice cream?"

"Sure. Don't you think we should?" I laughed to hide my admiration. "I mean, it would be rude to show up back at your place with ice cream and not bring her anything."

"You are too sweet." I put my arm around him and leaned my head against his shoulder. "I love how you always think of her."

"You seem surprised." He looked confused.

"I am. Most men don't consider their date's child when buying them ice cream at the end of the evening." I explained.

"Then they are not true gentlemen." He laughed without realizing the truth behind his statement. "Seriously, I just think it's rude not too. If you're going to date the parent, isn't it a package deal? I know your daughter isn't a child, but I want her to like me. I want her to approve of us being together." He gave me a gentle squeeze.

"You amaze me." I whispered softly.

Deuce was not my type — not in any way. Sure, he was good looking, but he was not the type I was usually attracted to. I usually dated men with white collar jobs; business professionals, lawyers, doctors. I definitely didn't want to get involved with a man who put his life on the line every day. I never wanted to sit at home and wonder whether he'd make it home from work that day. I didn't want to deal with the fear, the loneliness, the absent spouse on holidays. I wasn't sure if I could handle the aftermath of him emotionally dealing with the hellish nightmares he encountered because of his job.

And I most certainly didn't want to get involved with a man who had a minor child. True, I hadn't met Madelyn yet, but from everything I had heard about her mother I wasn't exactly excited about it. Hopefully, the apple fell far from the tree, but I had serious doubts.

I knew her mother was bipolar with a borderline personality disorder. Madelyn had a fifty percent chance of inheriting it from her mother. I knew the bipolar could be manageable with the proper medication and that her mother refused to stay on them or take them as prescribed. I also knew that no such medication worked on borderline personality disorder.

I was well educated in both. A doctorate in psychology told me what an uphill battle I would be charging into if I got seriously involved with this man. I knew the hell I was sure to face not just with Cathy, but with Madelyn also should she be unfortunate enough to inherit these disorders.

But I also knew it was too late for that. I was already in love with Deuce from the moment he showed up at my door on Tuesday evening and helped me with research. He was the most kind, generous, and loving soul I have ever encountered in this cruel world. He was the light of my life, and I knew I didn't want to live without him. Nor did I want to even try.

I already knew that no matter what the hell I had to face with his psychotic ex-wife and possibly with his daughter, I was willing to do it because I knew I would never find another man in this world like him. I knew there was no other man in this world like him.

~

The next evening, I slipped into a smoky, silk, nightie that hugged my curves perfectly. I brushed my long blond hair until it shone and cascaded over my shoulders.

I approached Deuce, who was lounging on my couch, reading a book. He looked comfortable, relaxed, and at home. I loved it. I lit several candles scattered around my living room. Then I pushed the button on the gas fireplace watching it ignite. I noticed his eyes following me about the room.

I turned and smiled at him, seductively over my shoulder, trying to tease him.

"Are you concerned about Brylee coming home?" A sly grin slid across his lips.

"Nope. She sent me a text that she'll be out with her friends tonight and is staying at Becca's."

"So, we have the place to ourselves?" His smile broadened.

"All night long." I motioned for him to come to me with my index finger.

"What do you have in mind?" Deuce rolled off the couch and crawled over to me.

On his knees, he took my hand and gently pulled me down to his level. His lips caressed mine. He nudged me down on the rug in front of the hearth.

Deuce's body slipped onto mine. His mouth tearing at me, hungrily with desire; he moved down to my neck and shoulders. His hot breath brushed across my skin, sending chills over my body. He tormented my breasts with his tongue, suckling them. I wanted him desperately.

His tongue played with my belly ring and traced along the top of my panties. I arched my hips towards him slightly, but he raised his head to shake it slowly at me in defiance.

Deuce stood up and removed his jeans and boxer briefs. He

stepped out of them and stood over me. I looked up at his gloriously well-developed body glistening against the flames from the hearth. His cock stood thick and firm at attention — all beautiful nine inches of it.

I loved his body. The mere shape of it. The strong muscular curves of it. The enticing way the glow of the flames reflected off it. The shadows that danced along the wall behind him gave his form a more mysterious and sensual mystique.

"I want you." I reached my hand up to him.

"I know." He said confidently looking down at me with a sly grin. "But not yet."

Deuce leaned over me and slipped my panties down my legs. He turned around over me and positioned his hips directly over my face; the head of his hard, beautiful dick touching my lips. I wrapped my fingers around the base and took the head into my mouth; teasing it with my tongue and sucking on the head of it.

I heard Deuce moan and felt his muscles tighten. He spread my legs further apart and drew my legs up toward him. He bent down and parted my lips with his tongue in one smooth, sensual motion that send shivers through my body. He licked my clitoris roughly, sucking on it, making me squirm beneath him. His fingers entered me slowly as I gasped for air. He probed deeper and deeper into me, enjoying the way my breath quickened.

I sucked on his thick cock with great enthusiasm. I loved the way it felt in my mouth. The sweet taste of him dripping from the tip of it. I licked it off eagerly. The head of his cock was perfectly shaped; full and broad. It slid down my throat easily as I sucked harder and harder, keeping the rhythm of it with perfect timing of the grasp of my hand stroking him from the base.

But despite the romantic ambiance of the roaring fire, the floor was hard and uncomfortable against my back with only the thin blanket as protection. Deuce must have noticed my inability to relax. He paused for a moment but didn't move.

"You're not supposed to be flinching." He half chuckled. "This is supposed to be romantic." I could see the smile on his face in the vacant space between us.

"The floor is killing my back. I'm sorry."

"Well, we can't have that, can we?"

Deuce lifted my hips upwards towards him and wrapped his arms around me. He moved his legs and got back on his feet. Before I realized what he was doing, I found myself upside down dangling in front of Deuce; my thighs resting on his shoulders, his cock in my hand.

"Oh, my God!" I squealed. "What are you doing?"

"You'd better hang on." He laughed. "I'm taking you to bed."

And with those words buried his face back between my legs and began licking my clitoris teasingly with his tongue.

"You're crazy." I giggled and wrapped one arm about his waist and kept one hand on the back of his throbbing cock. I tried not to laugh as I slid it back down my throat as he began walking through the house back to my room.

Sex with him is never dull!

Deuce kicked my bedroom door closed behind us and staggered over to the bed. He leaned over far enough until my back touched the comforter and in one swift motion, he pushed off the floor with his foot and slid me further back on the bed and climbed back over me.

It was the silliest, the sexiest, and the smoothest little trick I'd ever experienced, and I couldn't stop myself from laughing at his cleverness.

"You kill me." I said, still holding tightly to his dripping cock at my lips.

"I didn't want you to be uncomfortable or bruise that cute little ass of yours. So, don't say I never swept you off your feet. I just happened to be eating your delicious pussy while I did it." He chuckled with his face still buried between my thighs.

I could feel the vibrations of his laughter gyrating through me, and I couldn't help but giggle myself and try to squirm away from him.

"Where do you think you're going?" He scooted me back to him.

Deuce's fingers probed deep inside me, applying the perfect amount of pressure to my G-spot. His tongue lapped at my clitoris, stroking it firmly sending jolts through my abdomen down my legs.

I loved the way he knew just how to please me. He didn't have to search for anything. He didn't irritate me with his mind-numbing *one-stroke* like most men. And I certainly didn't have to fake anything with him.

A euphoric sensation flooded my brain and spread outward throughout my body all the way to my fingertips and toes. I soared off into another world on a cloud of pure adrenaline. I tried to hold onto it — that blissful high right before a full-blown orgasm raptures your soul.

My body twitched and flinched; my muscles spasmed uncontrollably. I tried to escape him, but Deuce wrapped his arms around my thighs and refused to let me go. I screamed out in pure pleasure. My nails scratched his chest, his abdomen, his back. I raked them over his buttocks and thighs, screaming out in pure delight.

Finally, Deuce relented. I collapsed back on the soft duvet completely spent. My breathing was labored, and I felt completely dehydrated.

"How was that?" He was smiling like a Cheshire cat.

"Oh, my God!" I ran my fingers through my hair that was damp with perspiration.

"Don't get too comfortable. I'm not done with you yet." He hopped out of bed; his silhouette against the light coming through the window was breathtaking. His perfectly formed, lean, muscular body crossed the room and walked out the bedroom door.

I stretched out comfortably across the mass of pillows at the head of my bed.

Deuce returned moments later with a water bottle for each of us. He handed mine to me, then plopped down on the bed beside me.

"Feeling better?"

"A thousand percent." I cracked open the bottle and gulped half of it down. "I needed that."

"The orgasm or the water." He eyed me curiously.

"Both." I giggled and grabbed the back of his hair, pulling him to me. "Definitely both." I kissed him roughly.

Deuce hovered over me; his naked body adorning mine with just enough weight to be sensuous. He positioned himself between my legs and nudged them further apart. His lips consumed mine breathlessly. He entered me slowly; gloriously filling me up. I loved the way his thick cock felt inside me. It was a perfect fit.

His rhythm was slow and steady to begin. His piercing clear blue eyes locked onto mine. My fingers ran through his short dark hair. He kissed me tenderly, softly, slowly; letting me know that tonight we were the only two people in this world. We were together.

NINE

I DREADED THE WEEKEND. After a blissful week in paradise beside Deuce, it was all about to come to a crashing end. Madelyn was coming home Saturday afternoon.

I had spent the last four nights falling asleep with my head on Deuce's chest, waking up with his arms wrapped around me. Now he was headed to some shopping mall parking lot on the north side of Phoenix to meet his crazy-ass ex and exchange his daughter. My dream had come to an end.

Shortly after Deuce left, I threw on a sundress and grabbed my sandals. With my hair up in a French twist, I picked up my car keys. I decided to run down to the store and pick up some groceries just to give me something to do. My mind was too scattered for me to concentrate on work.

With a bag of Oreos open on the passenger seat, I returned home. I brushed the Oreo crumbs off my dress and opened the trunk to retrieve my bags.

"Excuse me?" A voice coming up behind me caught me off guard.

"Huh?" I spun around with a mouth full of cookie.

"I know you don't know me, but I felt I needed to warn you." The tall, slender blonde woman began.

This stranger was slightly taller than me with dirty blonde hair, and a face that looked several years older than me. She was wearing faded jeans, ankle boots, and a maroon tank top with a plaid buttoned-up shirt that was unbuttoned with the sleeves rolled up to her elbows.

"About what?" I wiped the crumbs off my face with the back of my hand.

"I have been trying to reach my boyfriend, Grayson. I went to his house after work to talk to him, but he was pulling out of his driveway. I thought he was headed to the store or something so, I followed him. And he came here instead." She explained.

"Your boyfriend?"

"Yes, Grayson Steglich. We've been dating over three years now." She informed me.

"You must be Amber." I leaned against my car and sighed heavily. "He told me you broke up last December."

"We've had some problems, but we always work them out." Amber smiled sweetly at me.

"Have you spoken to Grayson since December?" I questioned.

"Like I said, we've had some problems, but we always get back together. He is mine. I simply wanted to let you know that he always comes back to me. I didn't want you to get attached to something that is nothing more than a fling to him." She stated in a snotty voice.

"I appreciate the warning. But I believe I will let Grayson make up his mind who he wants to be with." I turned around and started gathering my groceries. I shut the trunk and faced her.

"He's just using you. You must know that. We have a history and a future together. There's nothing you can do to change that.

I'd hate to see you get in over your head." Amber smiled sweetly and flipped her hair over her shoulders.

"Thank you for your concern. You have a wonderful day." I walked away without looking back.

I put the groceries away with my head spinning. I wasn't sure what to think. Deuce had told me he had split from Amber six months ago and hadn't spoken to her since. She had, as much, admitted the same.

But was there more to it? He said she wasn't nearly as crazy as Cathy, but after my encounter with her, I was now terrified to meet Cathy.

I wanted to call Deuce and tell him about my introduction to Amber. But he was so excited about picking up Madelyn, I didn't want to ruin his day.

I could only hope there was no truth to her words.

I knew what I felt like with Deuce. It was something I had never experienced before. I couldn't explain it, even to myself. I wanted to believe that he was experiencing the same feelings as I was. I just wish I could be sure, but there was nothing I could do because only time was going to let me know what his true feelings were.

~

Brylee knocked on my door about noon. She was dressed in her white bikini that left little to the imagination. Her beach towel was tossed over her arm, her hair pulled up in a cute messy bun. Only she could look so stunning in something so casual.

"Come lounge in the pool with me." I set my book aside and turned towards her. "It'll do you some good."

"It's miserable out." I complained.

"Hence, the pool. We'll float around and get a little sun." She grinned. "I even made a pitcher of strawberry daiquiri's."

"You're an angel." I climbed off the bed and headed into my closet to change.

We drifted around for a couple hours finishing two pitchers of daiquiris. Brylee was doing her best to keep my mind occupied. She knew what I was thinking and was polite enough not to mention Deuce the rest of the day.

We were feeling pretty good and looking bronzed by the time we headed inside. We took quick showers and put on some comfy pajamas despite how early it was in the evening.

While I was in the shower, Brylee had made popcorn and dumped in a bag of peanut M&M's. She made more daiquiris, loaded nacho's, and set up a tray of Red Vines — our traditional girl's night movie marathon paraphernalia.

"When did you do all this?" I joined her in the kitchen.

"I heard Deuce tell you he was picking up his daughter this afternoon and he would have her until Tuesday. Which means you won't see him until Tuesday." She reached over and put her hand over mine. "I went to the store after work yesterday. I figured you'd need a little break from reality for tonight."

I leaned over and hugged her. She was so incredibly sweet and considerate. I could not have asked for a better daughter. She had also grown into my dearest friend, and I loved this time with her.

"Okay." She let me go and bounced into the living room. "I picked out *Momma Mia* and *Rock of Ages* for tonight." She held up the two cases. "We'll start with *Momma Mia*."

I poured each of us another drink and joined her in the living room. Thirty minutes into the movie we were dancing and singing at the top of our lungs on the couch, jumping from the couch to the loveseat, and dancing across the living room with drinks in our hands.

We ate junk, laughed, and danced our troubles away. It felt wonderful to let all the angst go. I had spent the rest of the day since Deuce's departure, checking my phone every five minutes to see if he'd called or texted.

At nine, he hadn't.

It was just as well, I told myself. It was fun while it lasted.

I passed out shortly thereafter.

~

Sunday morning, I woke up at five feeling refreshed and rejuvenated. I pulled my hair up into a French roll and put on my golf tee and skirt. I brushed my teeth and splashed some cold water across my face.

Brylee was still sleeping, but I started the coffee, hoping it wouldn't wake her up. I took the first cup out on the balcony and watched the sun rise over the south mountain. It was a breathtaking sight and one that I dearly loved.

I met Shelly on the Bear Creek Golf Complex by six for our quarter past tee-time. She was already frazzled and rambling on about the crap with one of Brendon's exes. I would have exclaimed she had too much caffeine, but Shelly didn't drink coffee.

I, on the other hand, was already on my fourth cup. I placed my clubs in the cart and strapped them in. I climbed in on the passenger side, coffee and hand, and hoped Shelly was ready to get her game on.

Or at least what we considered game.

I left her to ramble on about her encounter with the ex and silently hoped I wouldn't be in her shoes any time soon. I barely heard her as my thoughts played out various scenarios with Cathy, none of which would be entertaining.

"Anyway, how did your date go with the cop?"

"Which one?" I smirked.

"Don't tell me you've spoken to needles?" She pulled up to

the fourth hole. "I thought you were done with him."

"I am. I was just kidding."

"So, how was the detective?" I stood back to allow her a couple practice swings before she teed off.

"Deuce was amazing." I hit my ball straight down the fairway. "We spent every day together since last Sunday." I walked back to the cart.

"And every night?" Her eyebrows raised.

"I did not say that?" I climbed in beside her.

"You didn't deny it."

"I did not sleep with him on the first date."

"Why not? I slept with Brendon on the first date." She shrugged.

"Well, I don't, and I didn't." I laughed.

"Don't judge me. He's amazing in bed." She smirked.

"Good." I shook my head with a smile. "I'm not judging."

"So, how was he."

"Amazing." I couldn't stop smiling.

"Really?" Shelly giggled. "Do tell."

For the next ten holes, I babbled on about Deuce and how wonderful he is. I told her about his romantic gesture, the silly movie he dragged me to, our endless night conversations, and finally admitted that I hadn't heard from him since he left my place yesterday.

"You're in love with him." She declared, pulling up to the fifteenth hole.

"I barely know him. It's been a week." I reminded her.

"And your point being?"

"Seven days, Shelly. I've known him seven days."

"You say that like it matters. When it's right, it's right. You can't explain it. You just feel it in your bones, your soul, your entire being." She reasoned.

"What are you smoking?" I shook my head at her. There was

no way I was going to admit I had already fallen for him.

"Wow. You're already gone." She laughed and pulled up to the next hole.

"Like it matters. He took last week off work to get some renovations done on his house while his daughter was in Wisconsin with her grandparents. She came home yesterday afternoon, and I haven't spoken to him since." I informed her.

"How old is his kid?"

"She'll be ten in September."

"A pre-teen. Oh, fun."

"I know. I've already raised two children." I smirked. "And I have no desire to raise another child."

"Look how many Brendon has, and I'm not running the other direction. And he has a true psycho ex." Shelly chuckled.

"Well, it seems Deuce has one of those himself. The stories he was telling me make my ex look like Prince Charming." I rolled my eyes in disdain.

"And you don't think he's worth a little aggravation?"

"Don't you mean a whole lot of aggravation? You consider his ex, who has been diagnosed with a bipolar and borderline personality disorder. A pre-teen daughter who may or may not have inherited the same disorders. A high-profile, stressful job that he's admitted has given him nightmares. Plus, Deuce was diagnosed with PTSD last December. That's a lot to willingly invite into your life, don't you think?" I looked over at her suddenly feeling very spent and it wasn't even noon yet.

"Didn't you say he was in the Marines?"

"Yes, in his early twenties."

"So, the PTSD is from working for the department?" She asked.

"Yes. And he sees a shrink."

"And now he's dating one." She grinned.

"I do I/O psychology." I reminded her.

"But didn't you say your bachelors was in psychology and your masters is in military psychology?" Shelly inquired.

"Yes, but I'm not a licensed psychologist. I never wanted to be. I mean, let's face it. I'd make the worst psychologist on the planet, and we both know it."

"Maybe. But you would understand what he's dealing with. You would be able to combat some of that for him." She reached over and put her hand on my arm. "Look. I know he has a lot of baggage, but you spent the better part of this morning telling me how amazing this man is. His baggage is nothing you can't handle with style and grace. I'm positive of that."

"I'm glad one of us is." Doubt crept into the back of my mind.

I was drenched in sweat by the time I got into my car. It was half-past ten, and I was wondering how Brylee was fairing this morning. She drank considerably more than I had the night before, but she was also 22 years younger than I and bounces back a lot quicker.

I pulled onto the interstate and tried to think of something we could do today together. Since we moved to Phoenix, Brylee and I had enjoyed going out and exploring new things or places. We would pick someplace either within the city or a day's trip from it and just go.

I wondered if she had looked up any new places this morning. She had mentioned to me last weekend that she wanted to go up to Payson and go cliff jumping. I'd done it before, years ago, but I wasn't so sure I could do it now. I knew if she urged me, I'd do it. But the truth was, I was terrified of heights.

But I would do it for Brylee, with Brylee.

My phone rang, breaking my train of thought. I answered it on my steering wheel.

"Hello."

"Hi, Arya. How was your game this morning?" Deuce's voice rang out through my speakers.

"Oh, Arya. I like you. I miss you." A little voice giggled in the background.

"Go clean your room." I heard a door shut. "Sorry. That was Madelyn."

"I figured as much." I couldn't help but smile.

"Are you headed home?"

"Yes."

"What's on your agenda today?" He asked.

"I don't know for sure. Brylee and I drank a little too much last night. I'm not sure what kind of shape she's in today."

"You were drinking with your daughter last night?" He chuckled.

"She's 23 years old. It was a girl's night."

"And girl's night with your daughter includes drinking?" He laughed at me.

"Drinking, junk food, dancing, singing. All the corny, goofy things we'd never do in front of men."

"Are you serious?"

"Yes."

"I would have loved to have seen that."

"Are you the one who's been telling me I need to relax a bit? I didn't do any work last night. If you'd have come by, you would have found me drunk, dancing and singing on my couch." I informed him.

"Oh, my God." He chuckled. "That's great."

"So, what are you up to today?" I tried to change the subject before he ridiculed me anymore.

"Just hanging around here with the munchkin."

"Brylee mentioned wanting to go cliff jumping up in Payson today. I'm not sure if she wants to go or not. We'll see." I pulled off the interstate and headed towards home.

"Cliff jumping? Really?" He sounded skeptical.

"I've done it before. It's not my favorite thing, but I'll do it for my daughter." I sighed.

"I couldn't do it." He stated.

"Can I get a snack." I heard a little voice pipe up beside him.

"Yes."

"Okay." Footsteps trailed off in the distance.

"By the way, I had a surprise visitor yesterday morning." I finally decided to tell him.

"Really? Who?"

"Amber — your Amber."

"What? How?" Deuce's voice took an edgy tone.

"Apparently, went over to your place to talk to you, but you were leaving. So, she followed you to my place." I told him.

"What did she say?"

"That you are hers and I'm merely a passing fling." I snorted in disgust. "She said you two were having a few issues, but you always go back to her."

"That was true, in the past. But no more. I told you I was done with her. I haven't spoken to her since last December. She's been calling me, but I haven't responded."

"Which is probably why she decided to show up at your place." I couldn't help but say.

"She lied to me, cheated on me, and then went on a cruise with another man a week after I flew to Seattle with her to meet her family." He sounded angry. "I have nothing to say to her."

"Okay." I was sorry I brought it up.

"And you're not a fling. You could never be a fling." He huffed. "You are so much more to me than that."

"I'm happy to hear that." It shouldn't have, but those simple words made me feel relieved.

"I'd like to see you." Deuce told me.

"I miss you." I confessed.

"Maybe I'll come over tonight after Madelyn goes to sleep. My mom will be here to watch her." He sounded hopeful.

"Do you think she would?" I hated to get my hopes up.

"Yes, I believe so." He paused for a moment. "Do you want me to come over?"

"Yes." I admitted.

"Are you going to let me spend the night?" He was toying with me now.

"I thought you had to work in the morning?"

"I work four tens, and I'm off on Monday's."

"Must be nice. Are you sure? I don't want to put her out." I hadn't even met the woman. The last thing I wanted to do was put her out for a booty call.

"No. She won't mind. She's actually happy that I've met someone who makes me so happy." My heart leaped up in my chest.

"I'd love to see you later if you can." I turned off my car and headed into the house. "You can go with us today if you want." I swallowed hard. "You can even bring Madelyn too."

"I don't think that's a good idea. I thought we'd agreed to wait on you two meeting for a few months or so and see how things go."

"Yes. You're right. You're right. I'm sorry." I opened the door and put my things on the kitchen table. "I'm not trying to push. It's been a long time since I had to worry about a little one." I tried to explain.

I glanced down the hall towards Brylee's bedroom. Her door was closed, and all was silent behind it. I crept into my room and closed my door softly.

"It's okay. We'll get there, Arya. I know we will." Deuce's voice was soft and comforting.

I stripped out of my golfing clothes and tossed them into the hamper. I put my phone on speaker and started the shower.

"Are you getting in the shower?" He asked.

"Yes. I feel nasty. I'm all sweaty from this morning. I stink." I pulled the pins out of my hair and shook it out.

"And you're keeping me on the phone, so I can sit here and think about you naked standing under the hot water covered in bubbles."

"Exactly." I laughed.

"You're so mean." I giggled again at him. "Evil."

I showered quickly and put on my red bikini with my pool wrap. I kept Deuce on speaker while I French braided my hair. I put on some sunscreen and brewed a fresh pot of coffee.

I spent the next two hours sitting on the balcony talking with Deuce waiting for Brylee to crawl out of bed. Our conversation was light and playful. We bantered back and forth, teased each other relentlessly, and laughed endlessly.

~

Brylee and I returned home a bit after dinner time. We were exhilarated, exhausted, and starving. Our scenic day trip up to Payson took more out of us than we expected. Deuce called us shortly after we descended out of the mountains and regained cell service.

I had him on speaker phone in my car, and he chatted with us the remaining hour drive home. He had Brylee laughing and giggling. She was completely enticed by his charms and was convinced he was the right man for me.

We stopped at In-N-Out Burger and picked up two doubles, fries, and chocolate milkshakes. We began stuffing our faces with fries before we made it home.

We showered and changed into comfy pajamas. Brylee put on a movie as I paced around my room, waiting for Deuce to arrive. His mother had agreed to watch Madelyn and take her to school in the morning, leaving us some much-needed time together.

TEN

THE WEEK FLEW BY BETWEEN work and Deuce. He stayed at my place every night and had practically moved in with me. I loved spending our evenings together, whether we dined out or I cooked, it was wonderful being with him. And Brylee adored his kindness and loved his sense of humor. It surprised me how quickly she took to him, considering she was more cynical and harder on men than I was.

I loved our playfulness. Never had I had a true partner, a lover, and a confidant. We wrestled, tickled, and laughed until we were in tears. And then made fierce love until wee hours of the morning. The sex was incredible. Deuce knew exactly what I wanted, how to touch me, how to make me scream at the top of my lungs.

Mostly, I loved falling asleep in the nook of his arm, nestled against him with my head on his chest. He had become the sun in my life, and the blanket that kept me warm at night. His strong and steady rhythm of his heartbeat had become my lullaby.

Wednesday morning Deuce texted me shortly after I arrived at the office.

'Good morning, sweetheart. I hope you made it to work okay. Ernesto is driving me crazy about meeting you. So, I was wondering if you wanted to get together for lunch?' He wrote.

'Hi, baby. I wish I could, but I already have plans for lunch with Shelly today.' I replied.

'ARE YOU SURE? She's not exactly appropriate lunch material. She's got the mouth of a sailor.' I told him.

'I guess you really haven't been around cops much. All of them have mouths that would make a sailor blush.'

'Okay. Spinato's Pizzeria on 7th Street and Missouri Avenue at noon.'

'Great. We'll see you there.'

I set my phone on my desk and pulled out my notes for my meeting this morning. I fidgeted with my pen and decided I'd best give Shelly a head's up. I picked up my office line and dialed her office number.

"Hey darling, how are you?" She picked up on the second ring.

"I'm surprised she's in this early." I teased. Shelly was notoriously late to work. She seldom made it into the office before eleven.

"I was interviewing a girl for the front desk position this morning at eight."

"Oh. That explains it." I chuckled.

"Very funny." She scoffed back.

"Deuce texted me this morning and said his partner wants to meet me. They invited me to lunch today."

"Is this your way of blowing me off to have lunch with some sexy men in uniform?"

"Okay. First off, they don't wear uniforms. They are detectives. Two, I wasn't blowing you off but asking you if you mind if they join us."

"That depends. How cute is his partner?" She sounded intrigued.

"Ernesto? I have no clue. I've never asked." I chuckled. "But I know he's about a year two younger than me. And aren't you still dating Brendon, or did you kick him out since Sunday?"

"Of course not. And seriously, they don't wear uniforms?"

"No. Sorry."

"Fine," she playfully huffed. "I guess I'll go."

"Fabulous. Thank you."

"I'll see you at noon." I hung up the phone and picked up my notes and headed out to my meeting.

~

Shelly was waiting for me in the parking lot when I arrived. Her long blond hair was blowing in the breeze, and she was struggling to keep her dress from flying up.

"Are you a sight?" I asked, walking up.

"Shut up." She smirked. "You look cute. I love that dress."

"Thanks. Are they here yet?" I opened the restaurant door for her.

"I don't know. I haven't seen Deuce, but I got here right before you."

I glanced around and then asked the hostess. She smiled and led us to a long table in the back. There was Deuce with several of his friends. He stood up as he saw us approach.

I was a bit taken aback. It was the first time I'd seen Deuce with his holster and weapon on. His badge was prominently displayed next to his right hip. He always removed them before he walked in the door in the evening and put them on after he left the house. I believe because he knew I was leery about dating an officer. It was one thing to *know* he was an officer; it was quite another to *see* it.

"Hi, darling." He leaned over and hugged me briefly. "This is Ernesto, Miranda, and Tony." I shook everyone's hand.

"Hello, it's nice to meet you. This is my friend, Shelly." She exchanged pleasantries, and we all sat down.

"I thought it was just going to be Ernesto." I leaned in and whispered to Deuce.

"Word got out that I was seeing someone, and they are nosey." Deuce said loud enough for everyone at the table to hear.

"I was just happy it wasn't Amber." Miranda pipped up with a cocky grin.

Miranda had long, wavy dirty blond hair and a cute smile. She was attractive with a feminine face but dressed in a buttoned-down shirt and slacks like the men. Her style was indistinguishable from the men's.

"Seconded." Ernesto added.

Deuce's partner, Ernesto, was a small Hispanic man that was maybe my height in my bare feet. He was nothing like the larger than life man I pictured when Deuce talked about him. He was cute in a more adorable kind of way.

"So, what do you do, Arya? Deuce doesn't tell us anything." Tony asked.

Tony was about a decade or so older than us with a cropped haircut and a potbelly. Out all of the detectives sitting at the table, he was the one that looked like a stereotypical cop.

"I'm an I/O psychologist; a business consultant and analyst." I shrugged.

"She's great. She completely restructured my company, and I've almost doubled my revenue in the last year." Shelly told them.

"Did you get your business degree for that or an MBA?" Tony asked.

"I got my doctorate in psychology." I replied.

"So, you're a psychologist as in with Ph.D.?" Miranda inquired.

"Yes, but I'm an industrial-organizational psychologist, not a clinical therapist. I work with businesses, not patients." I explained.

"What are you doing dating this three-headed monkey? You're way too intelligent to get involved with this idiot." Ernesto shoved Deuce playfully.

"I've told her that too." Deuce replied.

"He makes me laugh." I winked at Deuce. "And he's kinda cute."

"Really?" Miranda wrinkled her forehead and nose at me, making me laugh.

"Thanks." Deuce remarked.

"I'm sorry. I just don't look at you that way. You're like a brother to me." She shrugged with a coy smile.

"It must be really interesting being a detective. Are all of you homicide detectives?" Shelly asked.

"Yes." A chorus responded from the table.

Despite the next ninety minutes felt more like a panel job interview than lunch with friends, Deuce and I had survived the introductions. His fellow detectives were really nice and had the same sarcastic sense of humor as Deuce. Miranda and Shelly discovered they only lived a couple of miles from each other, and both had an affinity for riding their bikes in the evening for exercise. Before the luncheon was over, they had exchanged numbers and made plans to go riding together.

~

Friday arrived to quickly, and my heart sank to my feet. I knew I wouldn't see Deuce until Tuesday evening. I finished up a recap of the week on how implementing the new policy was going with the CEO and packed up my laptop. Renee, the COO, stopped by my office before I could escape.

"Got a minute?" She knocked on my doorframe.

"Sure. What's going on?"

"I wanted to let you know I won't be here on Tuesday. I have to be in court."

I knew very little about Renee, except that she was an exceptional worker, dedicated, and loyal. She was always very friendly, and her immediate staff loved her working with her. She was well respected by her superiors, and she had been my right-hand in the last couple of weeks since I started consulting here.

"Is everything all right?" I motioned to the chair across from my desk.

"Yes. I hope so. I have guardianship of my niece. She's two. My sister is an addict, and her father's in prison. I've had her since she was released from the hospital after she was born and detoxed from the drugs my sister pumped into her while she was pregnant. She's every bit as much my daughter as the two I gave birth too." She sat down and told me.

Renee was several inches shorter than I, and a bit heavyset. She had long red hair she typically wore in a bun, pale skin with light freckles, and a slightly crooked smile. She was cute and motherly. Her demeanor put people at ease. I could understand why she was so well liked and respected.

"Is your sister trying to take her back." I asked.

"No. I'm trying to adopt her. We did the home studies and jumped through all the hoops and such, and now we're hoping this is our final approval hearing." She grinned widely.

"That's wonderful. Congratulations."

"Thank you."

"Don't worry about anything Tuesday. You take care of your family."

"Do you have children, Ms. Lucas?" Renee asked.

"Yes. I have a son and a daughter. They are in their 20s now. My son is married and has a little boy that will be one in August."

"I'm guessing you aren't planning on having any more?" She chuckled a bit.

"No. I'm afraid that factory's closed. But the man I'm seeing has a daughter that's almost ten." I shared with her.

"And how is that going?" She raised an eyebrow.

"With him, it's fabulous. But I haven't met her yet. We've only been going out a couple weeks. It's too soon. We want to wait and see how things develop." I explained.

"And you're going to postpone the introduction as long as possible?" She chuckled.

"I'm just hoping she's nothing like her mother." I rolled my eyes and tried to smile. Sadly, it was the truth. I was scared to death of meeting Deuce's daughter.

"I understand that. My stepdaughter is fifteen, and she's a carbon copy of her mother. She goes out of her way to make my life difficult." The more people kept telling me about their experiences with stepchildren, the less appealing Deuce was becoming.

"I've heard they can be a nightmare. Which is why I don't really want one." I shrugged.

"Definitely something to think about before you get any more involved with him." She stood up.

"Believe me, I will." I stood up. "Thank you, Renee. I hope you have a great weekend."

"Thanks. You too."

Renee's words kept running through my mind as I sat in traffic, trying to get home. I wasn't excited to meet Madelyn even though she truly sounded adorable when she teased Deuce about me while we were on the phone. He had told me so many horror stories about Cathy, I did everything I could not to project my feelings towards Madelyn.

Deuce had told me about coming home and finding Cathy holding his six-month-old daughter and a 45 threatening to kill them both. And another time coming home to find blood up and down the walls along the hallway and her lying on the floor in a puddle of her own blood from slicing her wrists. She had gone nuts over him being assigned a female partner, called him excessively at work, and even made a scene at the precinct.

Apparently, those were some of her calmer days. The woman was a special kind of nut job.

My cell phone rang, breaking off my train of thoughts.

"Hello?"

"Hey, Arya. How are you?" Deuce's voice sang through my speakers.

"Good. How was your day?" I hated the way my heart leaped with the sound of his voice.

"It was okay. It's Friday, so I didn't do much." He laughed. "I picked up Munchkin, and we were trying to figure out what to do about dinner." He explained.

"I haven't even thought about dinner yet."

"I was hoping you'd say that." A knot developed instantly in the pit of my stomach.

"Why is that?"

"Because Madelyn and I wanted to invite you and Brylee to dinner tonight at Dave & Buster's. What do you think?" My mouth was dry, and I couldn't think of anything to say.

"I thought we had decided to wait." I managed to squeak out.

"I know. I know. But things are going great between us. Aren't they?" I heard a smidgen of doubt creep into his voice.

"Yes. They are." I inhaled deeply trying to gather my thoughts. "You were so against it before." I looked for any excuse I could.

"Look. If you don't feel comfortable with it, then we can wait until you're ready." The light tone he always had to his voice was strangely absent; telling me, I wouldn't easily recover his good graces if I didn't do this.

"No. I can do this." I swallowed hard. "I want to do this. Brylee and I would love to join you two. What time would you like us to be there?"

"How does seven work for you, ladies?" His voice immediately lightened.

"Seven's good. Tempe Marketplace?" I asked.

"That'd be the one." I could hear the smile in his voice. "I look forward to seeing you then."

"You too."

I hung up the phone on my steering wheel, sending a blast of the 80s back through my speakers. I wasn't sure whether I was ready for this. I had thought I still had some time, but apparently, the clock had just run out.

My phone rang through my speakers and for a moment I was hoping it was Deuce calling back to cancel because of something or other. But it was Ryan drifting back into my life from my past.

"Hello, darling. How are you?" His voice sounded cheerful and sexy.

"Hi. I'm going well. How have you been?" I was surprised to hear from him.

"Great. Working all the time." He chuckled. "But I'm off for the next seven days, doll. So, I thought I'd see what you're doing for dinner tonight. I've missed you."

"Ah, Ryan, I wish I could. But I already have plans for tonight." I confessed.

"Did you meet some hot guy while I was working?" The cheerfulness disappeared from his voice.

"Ryan, I haven't heard from you since February." I said in a light voice. "And yes, I met someone."

"Really? Who is he?"

"He's a detective with the Phoenix PD."

"Oh Lord, Arya. Seriously? Why would you get involved with someone who lies for a living?"

"He's not like that. I promise." I told him.

"They're all like that." He exhaled loudly. "I should know."

"I used to think that too, but I promise, he's not." I informed him.

"So, how long has this been going on?" He asked.

"Not long. Only a couple weeks."

"Oh, so it's not serious."

"I don't know." I confessed.

"Are you exclusive?"

"We haven't discussed it." I told him.

"Then, you're not. Okay. Well, dinner tomorrow night? I'll pick you up at six. I'll bring the Harley." I could hear the smile return to his voice.

"Ryan, I can't. We haven't even had that conversation yet. But I really like this guy." I realized at that moment that I didn't want another man in my life — ever.

Only Deuce.

"Then, talk to him. If you're not on the same page, then I'm picking you up tomorrow. I'll call you tomorrow afternoon." Ryan pipped up.

"You don't understand. I can't have that talk with him. It's too soon." I tried to reason with him.

"Just let him know if he's not going to man-up and make you his, then I will."

I couldn't think of anything to say.

"I'll talk with you tomorrow." And with that, he was gone.

~

Brylee and I arrived at Tempe Marketplace fifteen minutes early. The mall was packed as was typical for a Friday evening. I put the car in park and but made no effort to open the door. Brylee reached over and put her hand on mine.

"You can do this." She gently squeezed my hand.

"I don't want to do this." I looked over at her. "I can't do this."

"Deuce is wonderful. You really like him. He makes you happy. You know how long it's been since I've seen you smile like this?" I slightly shrugged. "Forever, mom. Forever." She raised her eyebrows at me.

"You realize this is the beginning of the end." I pointed out. "If she's anything like her mother, we're in for an endless nightmare."

"She's nine." Brylee laughed at me.

"And in a couple short years, she's got a fifty percent chance of turning into a psycho bitch like her mom." I shifted in my seat. "You realize there's a reason I never get involved with a man with minor children."

"And why is that?"

"We've been over this." I rolled my eyes at her. "Besides, I thought you enjoyed being the baby." I teased.

"I do. And I'm not about to relinquish my position to some little brat." She smirked. "Besides, she's his baby, not yours."

"It's sort of a package deal, you know. You get involved with the parent you get the kid as well. There's no other option." I leaned my head back against the headrest. "This sucks." I muttered, closing my eyes. "Let's go home." I started the car.

"No." Brylee reached over, turned it off, and stole my key fob. "We're doing this."

"Give me my keys." I held out my hand.

"I will. After we have dinner with Deuce and Madelyn." She opened her car door. "Come on, mom." She climbed out of the car and shut the door behind her.

"Agh!" I grunted loudly throwing opening my door. "You're

just mean." I slammed my door and walked around the back of my car. "I don't like you." I narrowed my eyes and glared at her.

"You love me." Brylee flung her arm around my shoulders.

"As long as you think so." I muttered giving her another playful dirty look.

Deuce and his daughter were waiting outside for us. Brylee saw them first. I could tell by her sudden intake of breath that caused me to look in the direction of where she was looking. She reached over and took my hand, squeezing it firmly.

But I thought she must be mistaken. Deuce was standing out front of Dave & Buster's, but not with Madelyn. She must have been bouncing around somewhere nearby. The child standing beside him was wearing a pair of old jean shorts, a gray tee-shirt, and sneakers. And was clearly a boy!

But I was wrong.

The little boy standing beside him was, in fact, his daughter, Madelyn. I had never seen pictures of her mother, but she resembled nothing of her father. She inherited Deuce's gorgeous blue eyes, but her brown hair had been chopped off into a little boy haircut.

When she smiled at us, I noticed the child had very protruding front teeth with a wide gape and was in dire need of braces. She walked hunched forward with her shoulders slouched in which made her bubble butt, the only other thing I could see she inherited from Deuce, even more prominent. Madelyn did not have a feminine bone in her body.

It's one thing to be a Tomboy; Brylee and I both could be considered Tomboys. We loved playing sports, target practicing, horseback riding, and our kickboxing classes. And while we both excelled at physical activities, we still did our hair and makeup every day and dressed liked ladies.

From what Deuce had told me, he had enrolled Madelyn in baseball, soccer, and basketball, but the child had no coordination at all. She fell over a flat service with nothing around her. She had also previously participated in gymnastics, ballet, ceramics, sculpting, coding, and computer graphic classes. None of which she showed any interest in and complained about endlessly. Currently, she was taking a theatre class.

I didn't know what to say. I painted on a smile and put one foot in front of the other.

"Here we go." I heard Brylee mutter under her breath loud enough for my ears only.

"Good Lord." I sighed and squeezed her hand again.

"Hi." Deuce greeted us as we approached. Madelyn hovered behind his back.

"Hello." My daughter and I said simultaneously.

Casual, but uncomfortable introductions were made, and the four of us headed inside. Brylee and I exchanged looks each knowing exactly what the other was thinking.

The hostess seated us at a table in the middle of the restaurant. Deuce and his daughter sat on a bench across from us in our chairs. Madelyn acted like any typical kid her age; she squirmed in her seat, insisted on ordering off the adult menu and then picked at her food, and literally hung on her dad's shoulder if not in his lap.

Brylee was pissed off because she had switched purses before we left and had somehow left her wallet on her bed. Therefore, she had no ID and couldn't get the drink she wanted. I ordered a Mai Tai and barely picked at the food in front of me.

Madelyn wanted to play some games after we finished eating. So, the four of us walked around the game floor. Brylee and I hung back while Madelyn dragged her father to anything that lit up and made noise.

We were bored senseless.

Anytime Deuce would try to get near me or talk to me, Madelyn jumped in-between us. She wasn't shy in the traditional sense, but it was apparent she wasn't comfortable either. I could tell she didn't like the idea of Daddy having another woman in his life.

Which was strange in a way because Deuce had told me that Madelyn was around his previous girlfriend, Amber that he had dated for over three years. He said they got along okay, but Madelyn had never really warmed up to her. He blamed it on the fact that Madelyn had such a strained relationship with her own mother and that Cathy didn't show the child any attention or affection.

It made me feel bad for the little girl.

Deuce and Madelyn walked us to my car at the end of our evening together. Deuce tried to take my hand but was promptly interrupted with Madelyn forcing herself between us again. I pretended not to notice, but Brylee rolled her eyes at me with a smirk.

"It was really nice to meet you, Madelyn." I smiled at her once we reached my car.

"You too." She grabbed hold of her daddy's hand and started pulling him away.

"Thanks for coming out." Deuce leaned over and embraced me. "I know it wasn't easy." He whispered in my eye.

"It was fun." I whispered back and kissed him quickly on the cheek.

"C' mon." Madelyn grabbed his arm and began pulling him.

"I'll call you later after I get this one in bed." Deuce winked at me and with a quick wave, was gone into the night being tugged off by the little girl on the end of his arm.

"That was fun." Brylee rolled her eyes again at me as we climbed into the car. "That was a girl?"

"Apparently." I sighed and started up the car.

"What's with the hair and the clothes?" She asked.

"I don't know. He told me her mom has no interest in her." I told my daughter.

"That's obvious."

"And sad." I glanced over at her as we left the parking lot.

"How can a mom not care about her kid?"

"I don't know, but there's a lot of them out there like that. Deuce said she's bipolar with a borderline personality disorder." I told her.

"Okay. Well, she needs to get help and be a mom."

"I agree." I turned onto the interstate. "He said she won't stay on her meds. She did some counseling when they were married, but it didn't last long because she didn't like what the therapist told her." I shook my head in disbelief.

"So, her mom is a lot like yours." Brylee dislike of my mother rivaled my own for a good reason. My parents spoiled my son rotten but barely acknowledged the existence of my daughter.

"Pretty much."

ELEVEN

RYAN CALLED AT SHORTLY before noon. I was finishing up some numbers and writing things done to go over with the accounting department on Monday. It was one part of my job. I let the phone ring three times before I picked it up. I wasn't sure what to say to him.

"Good morning."

"Hello, doll. How are you?" He asked.

"Finishing up some work. How are you doing?"

"You're working? Huh? I'm guessing you woke up alone?" He teased. "Did the exclusive conversation not go well last night?

"No, because I never brought it up. I told you yesterday, it's too soon for that conversation." I reminded him.

"You're scared." He laughed.

"No. I'm not." I lied. "We had dinner last night with his daughter. That was the first time I met her." I confessed.

"Good Lord. Seriously? He's got a kid? How old?"

"She'll be ten in September."

"Um. Did you forget your kids are grown? Why in the world

would you even consider walking into that nightmare?" Ryan inquired.

"I wish I had an answer for you. I honestly don't know." I sighed heavily.

"How did it go?"

"Honestly, it was awful." I told him.

"Do you really want to get involved with a mess like that? Having to deal with the kid? The ex? You finally got your freedom. We should be traveling together and having the time of our lives. You've already raised your kids. Do you really want to wait another decade to begin your life — again?" All valid points, I had to admit.

"Believe me, I've given it a lot of thought. He's an amazing man, and I really like him. I know it's a lot to take on." I hesitated a moment. "Besides, I don't even know where this is going."

"Meeting the kid pretty much means you're exclusive. You know that, right?" He stated.

"Yeah. I guess we did have that conversation after all." I sighed heavily.

"Yes. You did." Ryan laughed. "No worries, doll. I know you, and this won't last."

"What do you mean by that?" His words stung a bit.

"Arya, you never get serious with anyone." His voice was coy. "I've been trying for over a year to get you to be exclusive with me or even to take me seriously, but you push me away every time — granted, the morning after, but still." He teased.

"That's not true." I countered. "We've spent weekends together, even long weekends. I don't kick you out the morning after." I reminded him.

"But every time I mention anything remotely close about *us*, you change the subject and blame your career." He exhaled loudly. "So, once this guy pushes the subject with you, you'll disappear on him."

"That's not true." I stated with irritation because we both knew the odds were in his favor.

"Yeah, right. Anyway. I'll call you later." He laughed. "Have fun with your Private Dick."

"Very funny."

~

I spoke to Deuce for hours Saturday evening and Sunday but did not see him again until Sunday night. His mom had agreed to watch Madelyn again after she went to sleep so he could spend the night at my place. I hated to think about what this woman must think of me.

He called me Monday afternoon on my way home. It had only been ten hours since I'd left him sleeping in my bed, but I missed him terribly.

"Hey, doll. How was your day?" His soothing voice rang through my car speakers.

"Hectic. Yours?"

"I just hung out with the munchkin."

"Sounds fun."

"We were wondering what you and Brylee were doing for dinner tonight?" He asked.

"I haven't given it any thought. I haven't spoken to my daughter today."

"Is she at the daycare?"

"Yes. She should be home around six. I can ask her." I offered.

"Why don't you text her that we'll pick her up about six? She walked, didn't she." He knew her work was less than a mile from our home.

"Yeah. I'm pretty sure she did."

"Great. I'll meet you at your place at five, and we'll go get her." His voice was light and cheerful.

"Okay. I'll see you then."

I disconnected the call and turned up the radio. I dearly wanted to see Deuce, but I wasn't overjoyed about the prospect of spending another evening with Madelyn interrupting us every two minutes or forcing herself in-between us.

I exited the interstate and paused at the red light. I picked up the phone and sent Brylee a quick text. I told her we were going to pick her up and go out to dinner. She sent me back a smiley face in return.

They arrived shortly before five. I had just enough time to change clothes and take DaVinci on a short walk. Madelyn was dressed much the same as she was the first time I met her. She plopped down on my couch and picked up the remote and turned on my TV. I didn't say anything but gave Deuce a weird look. He shrugged it off.

We made small talk in the kitchen while Madelyn found some cartoons to watch. It was a bit awkward as I fiddled around not knowing what to say to her.

"Oh, I have something for you." I had almost forgotten.

"For me." Suddenly Madelyn remembered I was there.

"No, honey. For your daddy."

"Oh." She turned her attention back to the TV.

"It's in my room." I walked around the breakfast bar and headed back to my room.

"What did you get me?" Deuce paused in the doorway.

"It's silly, but I figured you'd need it since I've caught you several times waiting outside for me to come home." I reached in my purse and pulled out the key I had made for him at the hardware store on my lunch break.

"Seriously?" He looked down at the key and laughed. "Scooby Doo?" He shook his head at me but continued to laugh at the oversized Scooby Doo key to my home. "Are you sure?"

"I'm positive." I stood wanting to wrap my arms around him but didn't dare.

Deuce glanced over at his shoulder down the hall to make sure Madelyn was still watching TV. He stepped inside my room and quietly closed the door behind him. He walked over to me and pulled me close to him.

"You are amazing." He kissed me softly. "I am crazy about you."

"You're just happy I'm not crazy." I teased.

"True." He kissed me again. "But are you sure about this?" He nodded towards the key.

"I trust you." And I did. I couldn't explain it, but I fully trusted him with everything.

"I'd never do anything to hurt you." He whispered.

"Ditto." I kissed him more passionately.

"What are you doing?" Madelyn flung open my bedroom door and stared at us.

"Nothing." Deuce turned towards his daughter with a smile.

"I'm hungry. When are we leaving?" She stood there, eyeing me carefully.

"In just a minute. Did you turn the TV off?" He asked her.

"Okay." She hesitated in the doorway.

"Go." He raised his eyebrows at her, and she stalked off towards my living room.

"Sorry." Deuce leaned down and kissed me quickly.

"She doesn't knock?" I asked, slightly irritated.

"Oh. I hadn't noticed." He admitted.

"I did, and she needs to knock and wait for a reply before she opens any closed door in my house." I told him firmly.

"Okay. I'm sorry. It's just I've never enforced that rule in my house." He explained.

"Well, I do. And my children were raised to knock on a closed door and wait for a response before they open it. It's called respect for privacy." I stated.

"Okay. I'll talk to her." He kissed me again before walking out of the room.

I leaned against my desk and took a deep breath. I wasn't trying to be a bitch, and I felt like I'd snapped at Deuce, but I couldn't stop myself. I knew we had different parenting styles, but if Madelyn was going to be in my house, she was going to have to respect my rules. And a main one was respect for privacy and closed doors.

We took my car instead of Deuce's truck to pick up Brylee for dinner. I handed Deuce my keys as we walked outside. He just smiled, but I saw the surprised look on Madelyn's face.

Brylee was waiting outside when we arrived. She hopped into the backseat behind me and said hello to everyone. Her long hair was beautifully curled, and she was in a bouncy mood as usual.

"So, where are we going?" She cheerfully asked.

"What are you in the mood for?" I turned slightly in the passenger seat to see her.

"I'm hungry." Madelyn stated again.

"I know." Deuce told her. "What are you hungry for?"

"Food." She replied.

"How about Mexican?" I suggested.

"Fine." She sat back and crossed her arms.

"Which way?" Deuce asked.

"Just turn right." I told him as he pulled out of the parking lot. Brylee reached over the back of my seat and offered me her hand. I took it.

We made it two blocks. "Are we there yet?" Madelyn loudly asked.

Brylee squeezed my hand but remained silent, as did I. But I noticed Deuce grip the steering wheel a bit harder.

"Almost."

"I'm hungry." Madelyn stated again.

I turned towards the window and fought the urge to say something to his daughter; just as I'm sure Brylee was doing. She listened to whiny children all day as she worked in the four-year old's classroom. I knew listening to another one and not being paid for it, was not something she wanted to do.

Deuce pulled into Macayo's Mexican Table restaurant. He parked my car and turned towards his daughter. "We're here."

"Finally." She opened the car door and slammed it shut.

I took a deep breath and climbed out of my car. I closed my door and saw Madelyn run up to her dad at the front of the car and grab ahold of his hand. Brylee touched my arm.

I turned towards her, and she smiled and wrapped her arms around me in a brief hug.

"This should be fun." She whispered.

"Happy, happy, joy, joy." I snickered back loud enough only for her to hear.

She chuckled and took my hand as we walked towards Deuce and his daughter.

"How was work today?" I asked her.

"It was delightful. Henry was in rare form today. He bit three kids, so I had to write up a bunch of reports." She sighed.

"Ugh."

"How was your day?" She asked as Deuce held the door for us.

"Not much better than yours. Their accounting department doesn't bite, but they might as well. They are fighting the new software changes and making my life a living hell." I told her.

"There's always one." She was well versed in my dealings with resistance to change while restructuring organizations.

The hostess seated us in a corner booth. Brylee slid in one side, Madelyn the other. I slid in beside my daughter expecting Deuce to take a seat beside Madelyn who had scooted clear over to Brylee expecting the same. But Deuce slipped in beside me instead.

As soon as Madelyn realized it, she started sliding back out of the booth, but he stopped her.

"You're fine." He put his hand up and passed her the chips and salsas.

She gave him a dirty look but started stuffing her face. The waitress came by and took our drink order. The waitress barely got ten feet from us when Madelyn started in again about starving.

"You have chips. We'll order as soon as she gets back." He assured her even though the rest of us had barely picked up our menus.

Just to shut her up, Deuce ordered an appetizer for the table when the waitress returned so we could have a chance to decide what we wanted.

The evening started out rough and did not improve. Madelyn rarely stayed in her seat. She went to the restroom a couple times, bounced around, played with her food, and finally ended up standing next to the table hanging on her dad's arm claiming she was freezing.

Other tables were turning to look at us. I was so embarrassed. I had never seen a child of that age behave so badly in a restaurant. It was expected out of a two or three-year-old, but not a child three months from being ten. It was ridiculous.

We finished our meals as quickly as we could, paid the check and left.

We said goodbye outside my place. Deuce barely kissed me before being dragged off to his truck. I smiled sweetly and waved goodbye before taking a deep breath and closing my door behind me.

"What a freaking brat!" Brylee stated once the door closed. "Are you sure he's worth it?" She flopped down on the couch and closed her eyes.

"I'm not so sure anymore." I set my purse on the breakfast bar and sat down on the loveseat. "When it's just us, it's the most amazing thing. He's incredible, and I'm head over heels for him. But when she's with him, I don't even recognize him."

"Has he never heard of manners? Discipline?" She looked over at me. "Busting her ass maybe?"

"He needs too. That was embarrassing."

"Yes, it was."

"So, what are you going to do?" She asked.

"I don't know."

TWELVE

DEUCE WAS WAITING FOR ME at my place the next evening when I returned home from work. He was lounged across my bed still in his work clothes and stocking feet reading a book. I was delightfully surprised to find him there.

"How was your day?" I walked over to what had become his side of the bed and kissed him.

"Good." He smiled. "I wanted to see you. I'm on call so ..." His voice trailed off.

"So, you might get called out anytime." It was something I was still getting used to.

"Yep."

"Are you hungry." I sat down at my desk and slipped off my heels.

"A little. You?"

"Yes." I stood up and unzipped my dress. "I can cook tonight. I really don't feel like going anywhere." I tossed my dress into the hamper and put on my silk robe.

"Sounds good."

I cooked dinner for the three of us. Brylee got home a short while later and made blueberry muffins while I finished up the rest of the meal. Deuce was resting on the sofa with his feet up on the coffee table. He looked relaxed and entirely at home.

My daughter noticed me staring at him from the stove and reached over and touched my hand.

"Okay. He's worth it." She smiled and leaned over, kissing me softly on the cheek.

"Yes, he is." I smiled back at my beautiful girl. "It took me 45 years to find him, I'm not to give him up now.

After dinner, Deuce and I slipped out of our clothes and hopped into the shower together. My tub shower was much too small for both of us, and we playfully pushed and shoved each other to stand beneath the hot water.

"You think it's funny now, but it's not going to be when we end up in the emergency room with a cracked skull from falling out of the tub and hitting the toilet." I shoved him again and took back the hot water.

"No. Then it will be hilarious." He piped back and pinned me against the wall kissing me fiercely.

The hot water rained down on us as he lifted me up. I wrapped my legs around his waist and my arms around his neck, hoping to God he wouldn't slip.

Deuce maneuvered himself inside of me, crushing me against the cold, hard tile. His tongue searched my mouth eagerly. His grip bruised my ass with each hard thrust into me. He worked his way down to my neck, kissing my shoulder. I bit my bottom lip to keep from crying out in pain from the tile. His body stiffened as he came deep inside me.

I turned out the light and crawled into bed beside him. The soft glow from the television created a dreamy look on Deuce's face. He looked lost in his own thoughts as I snuggled up beside him. I rested my head on his chest and tossed my leg across him. He kissed the top of my head and stroked my hair.

"What's wrong?" I looked up at the profile of his face.

"Madelyn and I had a strange and sad conversation last night on our way home."

"How so?"

"Were you holding hands with Brylee in the car on the way to the restaurant last night?" He glanced down at me.

"Yes, why?" It wasn't what I was expecting him to mention.

"Madelyn saw you."

"And that was bad?" I shifted over to see him better. "I'm confused. It's just something Brylee, and I have always done. It's something we do as a way of comfort and strength." I shrugged. "I don't know. I guess I never thought it was unusual. Why? Did she mention it."

"Yeah. That among other things." He closed his eyes, looking exhausted.

"I don't understand why you're upset. What did she say?" I lightly ran my hand over his chest in a comforting manner. "Please. Talk to me."

"She noticed you two holding hands and hugging after you got out of the car. She heard you two talking about your days and laughing together." He told me but wouldn't look at me.

"Okay. What's wrong with that. We do that every day." I explained. "We're close." I hadn't given it any thought.

"Exactly." He leaned down and kissed my forehead. "Madelyn asked me how come her mother never holds her hand or asks about her day or hugs her." I noticed tears well up in his eyes. "My little girl asked me why her mother doesn't love her the way you love your daughter." He choked on his words a bit. "She wanted to know what was wrong with her."

"Oh, God." I whispered. His words ripped my heart out. "I'm sorry."

"Don't be. You didn't do anything wrong." He swallowed

hard. "I tried to explain to her that her mother has issues and that her mom loves her in her own way."

"I'm so sorry, darling. I wish I knew what to say." I wrapped my arms around him and held him tight.

I drifted off to sleep, knowing full well what Madelyn was feeling. It was the one connection she and I shared. My mother was very much like hers, and it was a horrible way for a child to grow up. It tore apart a child's self-esteem and left them with trust issues that lingered in the back of their minds for the rest of their lives.

I had barely survived growing up with my mother. I wouldn't wish that type of childhood on anyone. It was a rough way to start life.

~

Thursday evening, Deuce and I were lounging on the couch watching a movie. We were unofficially living together when Madelyn was at her mother's. I loved our time together and knew this was exactly where I wanted to be.

"What do you want to do about dinner?" He asked.

"I don't know." I hadn't given it any thought.

"What about some breakfast for dinner? Waffles, bacon, and eggs? Sound good?"

"It does actually." I admitted. "But I have no bacon." I sat up and turned towards him. "I can run over to Target and pick some up." I smiled. "It'll take ten minutes."

"Do you want me to come with you?"

"No. You look too comfortable." I leaned over and kissed his cheek playfully. "My lazy bum."

Deuce playfully shoved me away from him as I stood up. I laughed and picked up my purse off the bar.

"I'll be right back." I blew him a kiss before closing the door behind me.

I weaved through the crowd and purchased some bacon. I also grabbed a half gallon of Breyer's Drumstick ice cream because I knew it was Deuce's favorite. I retrieved the bag from the self-check-out and walked to the car paying little attention to anything around me.

"Does he ever go home?" I immediately recognized Ryan's voice.

"What?" I noticed him leaning against my car. His Harley was parked next to my car. "What are you doing here?" I shook my head with a grin.

Ryan's six-foot-plus stature was a commanding presence. His short, dirty blonde hair was slightly messed up from his helmet, and his Ray-Ban's hid his stunning green eyes. Several of his tattoos on his rippling tanned biceps were showing out of the sleeves of his worn red tee-shirt making him look even more sexy than usual. His torn, faded jeans fitted him like a glove. He was the epidemy of a hot bad boy.

Ryan was six years younger than me and enticing as hell. I hated to admit how much I desired him. His lustful appetite had no boundaries. He always kept life interesting, exciting, and adventurous — especially our sex life.

"Trying to find five minutes alone with you, but your Private Dick seems to be at your place every night this week." He rolled his eyes with a sly grin upon his shapely lips.

"He's not a private investigator. He's a Homicide Detective." I reminded him.

"Whatever." His cocky smile was infectious.

"So, why are you here? Are you following me?"

"Lovingly observing from a distance."

Damn that confident smile.

"You mean, stalking."

"Now that doesn't sound nearly as nice."

"Ryan. What are you doing here?" I opened the car door and set my things on the seat.

"I've missed you." He reached out and touched my hand. "Before you get in over your head with this guy, don't write me off."

"That's not fair." I whispered.

"Life isn't fair, Arya, but all's fair in love and war." He smirked. "Tell this Detective of yours that I'm not giving up." Ryan leaned over and wrapped his arm around my waist. He pulled me close to him and gently pressed his lips against mine. "I'm not going to give up until if or when he puts a ring on your finger." He kissed me again more firmly. "Maybe not even then."

I was stunned and speechless.

Without another word, Ryan got back on his motorcycle and fired it up. He put his helmet on, and with a cocky smile, he sped away.

"That was a long ten minutes." Deuce noted looking at his watch when I walked through the door.

"Sorry, I got hung up by an old friend." I put the almost melted ice cream in the freezer.

"And old friend? Who might that be?" He joined me in the kitchen.

"Ryan." I stated casually.

"Ryan? As in the Ryan that you used to sleep with?"

"That would be the one."

"And how did Ryan just happen to run into you at Target?" Deuce came up behind me and put his arm around my waist. He leaned down and kissed the back of my neck, sending goose-bumps across my skin.

"He didn't want to come to the door because she saw your truck was here." I explained.

"Do you still care about him?" He asked in a low voice.

"I care about him, but not in the way I care about you." I told him.

"You care about me?" A playful tone entered his voice.

"Yes. I suppose I do." I turned around and faced him. "A lot."

"Well, I suppose I care about you too." A boyish grin spread across his full lips.

"A smidgen, maybe?" I teased.

"Hum, maybe a bit more."

"Aren't I the lucky girl." I loved tormenting him.

Deuce reached up and touched my face lightly with his fingers. His face looked serious, but his eyes looked gentle, almost vulnerable.

"I love you, Arya." His voice was so low I barely heard him.

"I love you, too." I leaned up and kissed him softly.

After dinner, I left Deuce lounging on the couch while I slipped into the shower. I wanted to do something special for him. I dried my hair, put in a few loose curls, and applied some light makeup. I slipped on my garter with black silk stockings. I put on a black, pin-striped, corset, and tiny skirt that barely covered my ass that was designed to look secretarial. For added effect, I twisted my hair up into a loose French roll with one pin so I could take it out easily. I added some strappy-black stiletto heels and my glasses.

I twirled around in front of my mirror, making sure I looked sexy and seductive. I couldn't remember the last time I had done something like this. I had ordered the outfit last year as a joke when Brylee and I were goofing around online. It was my way of proving to her that I intended to date again someday and would, hopefully, find a man worthy enough to wear it for.

I took a deep breath and walked out into the living room. Deuce was snoozing softly with the remote lying in his hand. I smiled at the sight and gently took the remote from him. I placed it on the coffee table and carefully climbed over him, keeping my weight off him.

"Hey, doll," he stirred.

"Hi. You fell asleep." I leaned down and kissed him softly.

"You look incredible." He said in a low voice with a slight smile on his shapely lips.

"So, do you." I whispered.

"Yeah, drooling on your couch. Very sexy." His smile broadened.

"That's not what I meant. The sight of you in my home, sleeping on my couch. You belong here." I told him.

"I belong with you."

"Yes, you do." I kissed him again. "Come on." I climbed off him and took his hand gently pulling him up. "Let's go to bed."

"I'm exhausted." He moaned but followed.

"It's okay." I assured him with a wink.

"Arya?" He tugged back a bit on my arm. "I'm serious."

"I know." I led him over to the bed.

"I am exhausted." He flopped down on what was now his side of the bed.

"So, you said." I tried to straddle over his, but he stopped me. "What's wrong?"

"Please don't be upset. I'm just worn out. I'm not in the mood tonight. I just want to sleep." His dark eyes pleaded.

"Okay," I couldn't hide how much his words hurt.

"I'm sorry." He said as I walked into my closet in a vague attempt to hide my tears.

"It's okay. Really. I replied, feeling embarrassed and humiliated.

I quickly stripped off my outfit and threw it back on the top shelf. I swore to myself I'd never wear it again. I have never had a man turn me down before. I knew I shouldn't take it personally, but it was personal to me. After all that Todd had put me through, my self-esteem in this area was hanging by a thread.

Physically, people said I was attractive; that I looked a decade younger than my age. I had a thin waist and a great figure, but the years of living with Todd and his emotional brutality had taken its toll on me. If I gained three pounds, he not only noticed but made fun of me for it. If I did well in school, he took credit because he made dinner while I was studying. Nothing I accomplished in fifteen years was ever due to my own accord. He was responsible for all my achievements and was also the first to point out every failure or flaw as well.

I knew I was being ridiculous, and that Deuce was nothing like Todd, but I was devastated none the less. And it was not something I wanted to share with Deuce.

I put on a t-shirt nightgown and brushed my tears aside. I turned off the lights and climbed into bed beside Deuce and let the world drift away.

THIRTEEN

I WOKE UP FRIDAY MORNING knowing he was picking up Madelyn after work. I had reached the point where I dreaded and hated the weekends. I had quickly become so accustomed to falling asleep beside him, seeing him in my home, having him in my life. I hated that it was only on a part-time basis. I wanted more.

I spoke to him briefly after I got off work, but he was busy with Madelyn and got off the phone quickly. I didn't think much of it and took advantage of Brylee being home for the evening. I decided to take her out to dinner and spend some time with her. I felt like I hadn't seen her all week.

We ended up at Texas Roadhouse for the cinnamon butter and hot rolls. She and I loved them. I told her about my late-night conversation with Deuce about Madelyn and how bad I felt for her.

"I understand why you feel bad for her, momma. I do too. But that doesn't excuse her behavior. The child needs manners." She took a bit and raised her eyebrows at me.

"Agreed. And structure, consistency, and discipline." I tore a piece of roll off and popped it in my mouth. "I don't know if I have the patience." I let out a deep breath.

"You're in love with him." She smirked.

"I know, but I don't know what to do about it."

"Aren't you the one who told me it's a package deal?"

"Yeah, but that's a huge package, and you know it." I reasoned. "I don't expect anyone to be perfect by any means, but is it too much to ask for a child that doesn't behave like she was raised by wolves?" I only half chuckled.

"I've never seen you so happy. And he's clearly in love with you too." Brylee smiled. "You deserve to be happy, momma."

"So, do you." I reached across the table and squeezed her hand.

"We'll see." Thanks to her dad, my horrible relationship with him and a couple rotten boyfriends of her own, my beautiful daughter was more cynical about happily ever after than I was.

"Are you two getting serious?" She asked.

"I think so. Why?"

"Because I've still got a couple years left of school and I was thinking of getting my own place." She explained.

"I thought we'd agreed to live together until you were done with college."

"I'm around kids all day. I really don't want to live with one." I hadn't thought about that.

"I understand, but darling, we've only been dating a couple weeks. The idea of us living together or more is a long way down the road." I assured her. "I'm not ready to jump into something like that. I treasure my freedom too much; especially after how hard I had to fight to get it."

"Are you sure?" I nodded.

"Positive." I reached across the table and touched her hand. "I don't want you to move out. You have enough on your plate, and you don't need to be worrying about making rent or utilities."

"Okay." She smiled. "I just wanted to make sure."

~

Deuce called me first thing in the morning on Saturday. Brylee was still asleep, and I was out on the balcony enjoying the sunrise with my first cup of coffee.

"Good morning, darling." It felt wonderful to hear his voice.

"Good morning. How did you sleep?"

"I sleep better with you beside me." I admitted.

"I know. I do too."

"What's on your agenda for today?" I asked.

"Not much. I'm on call, so I really can't do anything. But I was thinking about going out for breakfast. Would you ladies care to join us?"

"Brylee's still asleep." I was hoping that would get us out of it without sounding rude.

"What time do you expect her to wake?"

"It's Saturday. There's no telling." Which was the truth.

"Can you wake her?" He asked.

"Have you met her?" I laughed. "She's not exactly a morning person." That was putting it mildly.

"Fair enough. Do you think she'd be ready by nine?"

"It's doubtful she'll be functioning by noon." I said honestly.

"Well then, would you like to join us?"

"I'd love too." I went inside to fetch another well-needed cup of coffee. "What time?"

"We'll pick you up at nine."

"Sounds good." The clock on the stove said it was half-past seven. "I'll be ready."

"Bye." He disconnected the call, and I set my phone on the breakfast bar.

"Ready for what?" Brylee's sleepy voice entered the kitchen. "Is there any coffee left?"

"Yes. Deuce invited us to breakfast." I told her.

"With him and the monster?"

"Yep." I added some creamer to my coffee. "Want to come?"

"I'll pass." She walked into the living room and curled up on the couch with a blanket.

"Please. Come with me." I walked over and joined her on the other end. "Don't make me face this alone." I pleaded.

"You won't be alone. Deuce will be with you." She gave me a cocky smile.

"You know what I mean." I complained.

"Is he going to put her on a leash?"

"I seriously doubt it." I took another long drink of my coffee, hoping it would give me strength.

"Then, no." She flipped on the TV as her way of telling me the conversation was over.

"Please, Brylee. Don't make me go alone." I begged. "I need you."

"What's in it for me?" She loved to play her little games.

"You can shower first." I offered.

"What time are they invading?" She huffed.

"Nine."

"Good Lord." She kicked off the blanket. "Fine. But you owe me."

"I know."

"And I'm taking a shower first." She reached her doorway but turned back towards me and stuck her tongue out with a smirk. "And I'm using all the hot water."

"I figured as much." I heard her chuckle as she closed her door. "Thank you!" I hollered after her.

They arrived promptly at nine. I was finishing up my makeup when they arrived, so Brylee let them in. I heard them exchange pleasantries and then a moment later Brylee walked in my room with her jaw clenched and teeth clenched together.

"I'm going to kill her." She stated hatefully.

"What did she do now?" I huffed.

"I was watching a show, and she just picks up the remote as soon as they walked in the door and changed the channel." She narrowed her eyes in anger. "She didn't even ask, and he didn't say a damn word."

"Calm down." I put my hand on hers and gently squeezed it. "I'll take care of it."

I leaned out my bedroom and asked Deuce to come here for a moment. He got up from the couch and passed Brylee on her way to her room. She shut her door loudly as he entered.

"Good morning." He immediately leaned over and kissed me.

"Hi, baby." I hated this. "Can you please close my door?"

"What's going on?" He looked confused.

"Have a seat." I waved at my desk chair.

"Okay." He hesitated for a moment but then walked over and sat down.

"We have a problem." I sat down on the corner of my bed across from him. "Twice now Madelyn has entered my home, and without permission, she's flipped the channel on my television. I didn't say anything the last time, but today, Brylee was watching something."

"Oh."

"And she's pissed."

"I'm sorry. I didn't even think about it." I tried not to ask him how he could not.

"Brylee has an older brother that she grew up tangling with. I'm telling you now because I don't want my daughter to thump on your daughter." I playfully told him hoping he would catch the serious undertone to my words.

He didn't.

"All right." He looked embarrassed.

"What'cha talking about?" I spun around to the sight of Madelyn walking in my room.

"Have you ever heard of knocking first?" I blurted before I could stop myself.

"What?"

"Knocking on a closed door?" I took a deep breath. "This is my bedroom and my house. You do not open a closed door in this house — ever!" I kept my voice calm and even trying not to express the anger that I was feeling boiling inside me. "You knock first and wait for someone to reply. Then after permission, you can open the door. If they tell you they are busy, you do not open it. Do you understand me, Madelyn?"

"I don't have to knock." She looked over at her dad.

"That may be the rule at your dad's house, but this is my place, and it's called respect. You show respect in my house by knocking on closed doors. Understand?" She nodded slowly, still looking at her dad to say something.

He didn't.

It was then that I noticed she was wearing a white tee-shirt with some funky design on it. But that wasn't what caught my attention. Deuce's little girl was developing, and her little breast buds were very prominent through her shirt.

"Go back into the living room. We'll be out there in a minute, and then we'll go get some breakfast." Deuce instructed her.

"I'm hungry." She stated before she left the room, leaving my door open.

"We need to stop by Target before we go anywhere." I got up and closed the door once more.

"For what?"

"A bra for your daughter." I told him.

"She has some." He looked puzzled.

"Go out there and look at your little girl and then tell me we don't need to stop by the store before we eat?"

"Fine." Deuce got up and walked out of my room.

This is going to be a long day.

I returned to my vanity and finished messing with my hair. I slipped into my sandals when Deuce came back in with an annoyed look.

"Okay, fine. We need to go by the store before we eat."

~

Turns out a training bra wasn't the only thing we needed to pick up. Apparently, his little girl couldn't remember to shave under her arms or put deodorant on either. We also picked her up a couple pairs of pajamas and a new bathing suit simply because they were on sale.

We had left an annoyed Brylee at home because Target was just around the corner from our place. Her mood hadn't improved much, and she reminded me again that she wasn't happy and wanted my permission to thump Madelyn. After her behavior at the store and whining to get Deuce to buy her anything she wanted and him doing it, I was on the verge of giving it to her.

I wasn't sure if I was strong enough to do this.

Breakfast was no better than dinner with her. She behaved much the same. This time we had the pleasure of sitting at a table with four chairs right in the middle of the restaurant. She was up and down, running to the bathroom, hanging on Deuce's arm, and pulling on his arm trying to get into his lap because she said she was cold.

Same as before, people around us stared and whispered. Brylee and I both ordered a mimosa trying to maintain our composure. We'd both finished off our second one before the meal was over.

I felt so torn. I rested my head against the window on our way back to my place, wracking my brain about how to handle the situation. Brylee was miserable, and I understood why.

Deuce was the most incredible man I had ever met. He was kind, loving, sweet, and considerate. And utterly blind to the inappropriate behavior of his daughter. I wasn't sure I was up for this type of battle.

Deuce's phone went off, breaking my train of thought. Multiple text messages came through almost on top of each other, which put a knot in the pit of my already queasy stomach. When the ringing started seconds later, I knew it was bad.

"Okay." He paused to listen. "Yeah. I'll be there shortly." He hung up and dropped the phone in his lap.

"I have to go into work." He looked over at me.

"I figured as much." He pulled up to my place.

"I have some clothes here, right?" He parked the car and glanced over at me.

"Yes. I washed them and hung them up." I half smiled.

"Okay, thanks. I wasn't sure. I brought some with me just in case." He patted my hand and got out of my car. "I just need to change real quick."

I followed him into the house, trying to figure out what his plan was for Madelyn. I knew his mom usually watched her when he got called out. He unlocked my door and held it open for the three of us.

I put my purse on the breakfast bar and headed into my room to show Deuce where his clothes were. I pulled them out of my oversized closet and laid them out on the bed for him. He was already undressing.

"What are you going to do with Madelyn?" I nonchalantly asked.

"Um. I guess I can drop her off with my mom." He fumbled with his pants. "Let me call her and make sure she's home. She knows I'm on call so she should be around." He started looking around for the dress shoes he left on his side of my bed. I went to the closet and brought them out, setting them before him.

"Oh, thanks." He slipped them on.

He dug his phone out of the pocket of the jeans he'd left casually on my floor without a second thought. I cringed and looked at them lying four feet from the hamper.

His mother never answered.

He waited for two minutes and tried her again.

No answer.

"Look. I've got to get out there. Would you mind keeping an eye on Madelyn for me?"

Damn it!

"I should be back in a couple hours. I'm not sure exactly what's going on, but I'll call you as soon as I get there."

"Of course." He wrapped his arms around me and pulled me close.

"Thank you."

I was terrified to go out there and tell Brylee that Deuce was leaving, and Madelyn was staying with us for the day. She was going to kill me.

Deuce got his bag and kissed his daughter and me goodbye. As soon as the door closed behind him, she plopped back on the couch and turned on the television. Brylee glared at me and went into her room and closed the door.

I stood in the foyer and took a deep breath. I barely knew this kid, and from what I did know, I can't honestly say I liked her very much.

A part of me felt bad for some of the things she was dealing with. The other part of me saw the spoiled, ill-mannered, disrespectful brat.

"What would you like to do, Madelyn?" I tried to sound cheerful as I walked over to the couch and leaned on the arm.

"Nothing." Her eyes never left the television screen.

"Wonderful." I clapped my hands together. "Your dad just bought you a new bathing suit." I pulled it out of the bag she'd left on the end of the couch and tossed it at her. "There's the bathroom. Go put it on."

She looked at me but didn't say anything. A moment later, she turned her attention back to the TV. I stood up, walked over, and turned it off.

"The bathroom is right there." I pointed.

"Fine." She picked up the suit and stalked off.

I shook my head slightly and walked over to Brylee's door and knocked softly.

"Brylee? Can I come in?"

"Yeah." I opened her door and closed it behind me.

My daughter was lounging on her bed, reading a romance novel.

"Did he get called out?"

"Yeah."

"And Madelyn's here?"

"Yep." I sat down on the side of her bed.

"For how long?" She set her book aside.

"I don't know." I shrugged. "He's supposed to call me when he has an idea. Want to go out to the pool with us?"

"Nope."

"Please."

"I've had enough for today." She picked her book back up.

"I understand." I walked back over to her door. "So, have I."

I closed her door and went back to my room. I changed into my white, pink, and black bikini and tied the sheer wrap around my waist. I grabbed my sunglasses, phone, and slipped into my flip flops and went in search of my afternoon companion.

I didn't have to search too hard. She was right where I thought she'd be — in front of the television.

"Madelyn?"

Nothing.

"Madelyn?" She finally turned towards me. "Did I say you could turn my television on?"

"What?"

"You heard me." I tossed her a beach towel and flipped the TV back off. "C' mon.".

She reached over to pick up her little squishy toy when I noticed her arms. I wasn't sure if I should say anything or not, but I decided I had too.

"Madelyn? Um ... honey, are you shaving your arms?"

"Yeah, sometimes."

"Come here, sweetie." I stood up as she approached me. "Can I see?" She lifted her arms for me. It looked like she'd been shaving her arms with a weed-wacker. "Oh, darling." I put my arm around her. "C' mon." I led her into my bedroom.

I stood her in front of my vanity and got a new razor out of my linen closet.

"Has anyone shown you how to properly shave your arms? Your mom maybe?" I hated to ask because I already knew the answer.

"No. She just handed me a razor and told me to shave my arms." Madelyn suddenly looked like a lost little girl, and I felt horrible.

"Okay." I patted her shoulder and got the shaving cream out of my shower. "Thankfully, you're in a bathing suit. We can do this." I smiled at her.

And for the first time, she smiled at me.

I lathered up her arms and showed her how to properly shave them. I did one and watched her as she did the other. She asked questions but was grinning from ear to ear. She even giggled at one point.

Maybe she wasn't Satan in a bowl haircut after all.

"All right. I think we're ready." I finished rinsing her off and then tossed her the sunscreen. "Put some of this on before your dad screams at me if you get a sunburn."

"Okay." She started smearing it over her arms.

"I'll put a little on your back." I told her before I did.

"Thanks." She shocked the hell out of me.

I heard my phone buzzing from the living room. "Oh, hold on." I grabbed a towel and ran out of the room.

"Hi, baby." Deuce greeted me. "How're my girls?"

"We're making daiquiri's and heading out to the pool?" I walked back into my room. Madelyn giggled at me.

"Shouldn't you wait until I get back?" He sounded leery.

"Wait for what? The daiquiri's or the pool?" I teased.

"Um. Daiquiri's, I guess." He laughed. "Oh, and please make sure you put sunscreen on her. I don't want to listen to her mother bitch if she gets burned."

"I already did." I said with a coy tone. "Believe it or not, I've done this before."

"I know. If I didn't trust you, I wouldn't have left my daughter in your care."

"I promise I'll take good care of her."

"I know you will." He sighed. "It looks like I'm going to be here for a while. We've got multiple bodies, gang shooting. I'll be lucky to be out of here before dinner."

"No problem. Madelyn's fine."

"Yeah, dad. I'm fine." Her small voice added to the conversation.

"Okay. I'll call you later when I know more. Have fun."

"You too." I chuckled.

"Yeah, right." He hung up the phone.

"You ready?" I asked the new little lady in my life.

"Yep." Thankfully, her attitude seemed to have shifted.

Madelyn and I went out to the pool and tossed the rafts in the water. It was in the high nineties, and there wasn't a cloud in the sky. The palm trees were swaying in the light breeze high above the clear blue water.

We descended the steps into the cool water. Even without a heater, the pool waters in Phoenix by this time of the year were losing their chilly effects and had moved into serving as a way to tolerate the heat while outside.

Madelyn was telling me about how much she enjoys spending time in the pool at her mom's place. Her mother's third husband had a daughter two years younger than Brylee, and the two of them liked to sunbathe together when she visited. She climbed up on her raft and continued to ramble on about school and her other family. She talked nonstop.

"Do you and my dad have sex?" I was floating around half listening to her when those words caught my attention.

"What?"

"Do you and my dad have sex?" She repeated.

"You shouldn't ask me such questions." I shifted my raft to face her. "Do you even know what sex is?"

"Yes. My stepsister, Cassey, lets me watch movies with her. I've seen it." She informed me.

I wasn't sure exactly what she'd seen or the type of movies her stepsister was allowing a nine-year-old to watch, but I didn't think it was anything Deuce was going to approve of.

"Does your mom know that Cassey lets you watch those movies?"

"Yeah." Madelyn shrugged. "She doesn't care. She took me to see *It* last summer, and I've seen all the seasons of *American Horror Story*."

"Are you serious?" She nodded. "I don't watch those things. They give me nightmares." I told her honestly.

"Me too, sometimes." She admitted. "Are you getting serious with my dad? Are you going to marry him?"

"We are together. Your dad makes me very happy."

"Oh." She looked down and fidgeted with her fingers.

"But you know. Your daddy loves you very much, and he talks about you all the time." I told her.

"Really?" Her face brightened.

"Of course." I smiled over at her. "You know you're the most important person in the world to him. I'm not trying to take your daddy away from you. I'd never do that. I just want to make your daddy as happy as he makes me."

"That's good. I want him to be happy too." She smiled. "Does Brylee like my dad?"

"Yes. She likes him very much."

"She likes you too." I could see where she was going with this.

"She's very special."

"You love her?" She stared at me.

"Yes, more than life. She's my baby girl."

"You two are a lot alike." She observed. "Do you spend a lot of time together?"

"We try to. It's hard between work and school, but we try to spend one day a week together to catch up and do something fun." I explained.

"My mom doesn't do that. She thinks I'm stupid and I stink." Her head dropped forward.

"I'm sure she doesn't think that." However, I wasn't sure at all.

"Yes, she does. She told me." Madelyn said, barely loud enough for me to hear her.

"Madelyn?" She looked up at me. "Your daddy told me that your mom has issues and sometimes she says things and does things that aren't very nice." She nodded. "I understand how she makes you feel. My mom was a lot like yours. So, I do know what you're going through. It's really hurtful when someone who is supposed to always be there for you, isn't or when they say things to you that hurt your feelings and make you feel small."

"Was your mom like that?" She asked.

"Yes. And she still is. It's hard for me to talk to her, even today." I confessed.

"I don't talk to my mom much." Madelyn fidgeted.

"I'm sorry."

"But you and Brylee aren't like that." She observed.

"No. So, as you can see, just because your mom is like that, it doesn't mean you will be like her when you grow up." I assured her.

Madelyn smiled at me with the warmest eyes. She finally understood she wasn't destined to follow in her mother's footsteps. I believe she felt relieved.

FOURTEEN

DEUCE SHOWED UP BACK AT my place shortly after I tucked Madelyn into bed on my sofa. He looked exhausted and weary. His sleepy eyes glistened a bit when he saw his daughter sleeping soundly in my home. He showered quickly and fell into bed.

I snuggled up against him and rested my head upon his chest. I took a deep breath, satisfied that he was finally home. I worried about him constantly when he was out on a call. I knew he arrived *after the scene of the crime*, but that fear remained in the pit of my stomach.

"How are you feeling?" I traced my fingers lightly over his abdomen.

"Drained." He sighed heavily.

"It's been a long day." I agreed.

"How was munchkin?"

Before I could respond, Deuce's phone went off. He glanced down at it and declined the call. Annoyed, he put his phone face down on the nightstand beside him.

"Who was that?" I asked, although something in my gut told me already.

"Amber." He rolled his eyes.

"She's persistent." I muttered. "Munchkin was great. We went swimming, watched a movie, and had pizza for dinner. She took a shower and then fell asleep a while ago."

"That's good." He squeezed me a little tighter. "Would you mind getting me a bottle of water?"

"Not at all." I climbed out of bed and went to the kitchen.

Deuce was holding my phone when I returned. He was texting someone with a scowl on his face. He finished whatever he was typing and tossed my phone on my pillow.

"Did someone text me?" I asked as I handed him the water bottle.

"I wish they'd get it through their heads that we're together." His voice was curt.

"Huh?" Confused, I picked up my phone and checked my messages.

The last message I received was from two minutes ago from Ryan. It simply read; *thinking about you.* Deuce had responded with; *I'll be thinking of you tonight when I stick my cock in her.*

"Seriously? Do you feel better?" I put my phone back on my nightstand and flopped down on the bed.

"He needs to understand." Deuce's voice was harsh.

"Oh, and have you had the same conversation with Amber because she seems to be failing miserably at the whole understanding thing." I informed him.

"I broke up with her in December. I made it perfectly clear to her. It's not my fault; she's an idiot and can't let go. But have you told Ryan the same thing?" he asked.

"Yes, a couple of times."

"Then don't get upset with me for reiterating it because he obviously didn't hear you." Deuce told me.

"Don't you think your response was a tad juvenile?" I couldn't hide the sarcasm in my voice.

"No. I thought it was funny."

Somehow, I didn't think Ryan would. And I knew I shouldn't care about how Ryan was feeling, but he was a friend and someone whom I'd known for well over a year. We had spent a lot of time together, and while I wasn't in love with him, I certainly didn't want to hurt him.

"Then perhaps the next time Amber calls or texts, you allow me to return the favor." I reached over and turned off the light.

It was our first disagreement. I felt both horrible and exasperated. I wanted to roll over and snuggle up to him like I always do, but he had turned his back to me.

Seconds later, he was snoring.

~

The fourth of July landed in the middle of the week. For the last several months Brylee and I had made plans to go to Lake Tahoe. We had rented a cabin and were meeting my son and his family there for a getaway vacation for all of us. I was so excited to see my grandson, Sawyer, and spend some time with Carson and Alicia.

Since Carson had joined the military, he had been stationed in three different garrisons and deployed twice. I had mentioned the trip to Deuce a couple weeks ago, but somehow it had escaped his memory with all we had going on until he came home and found my suitcase lying across my bed and clothes scattered about.

"Are you going somewhere?" Deuce set his work briefcase down by his nightstand.

"Yes. Lake Tahoe. Remember?" I placed several pairs of

shorts in my bag. "I'm meeting my son and his family up there for the Fourth."

"Oh, yeah. I remember you saying that." He sat down in my desk chair.

"Are you upset?" I went over and sat on his lap.

"No. I've just gotten used to coming home to you every day. I'm going to miss you." He pulled me close to him and kissed me.

"I'll only be gone for ten days."

"Ten long days."

"I'm going to miss you too. I wish you were going with me."

"Me too. I've never been there. I would love to go." A sweet smile shown across his shapely lips.

"We do this every year, so hopefully next year you can go with us." I kissed him again.

"Well, I'm not going anywhere." He held me tight.

"Does that mean you plan on being around for a while?"

"A long while."

That evening, I snuggled into bed beside Deuce and wrapped my arms around him. I hated the thought of leaving him. It had barely been a month since he'd entered my life and I couldn't imagine my life without him. I found it hard to sleep on the nights he spent at his place. Lately, I've found myself fantasizing about the day when we would never have to spend a night apart.

I didn't care if we ever got married. I simply wanted to spend my life with him.

Deuce nestled up behind me and wrapped his arm around my waist. His lips brushed the back of my neck, his breath hot on my shoulder. I closed my eyes and pulled him closer to me.

"I love you." His voice was soft.

"I love you, too."

He traced his fingers lightly over my shoulder and down my arm. His lips brushed softly over my shoulder. He ran his hand down to my hip and squeezed me gently.

"What am I going to do without you for ten long days?" He whispered.

"Work. Spend too much time talking to me on the phone." I nuzzled against him. "Miss me."

"I guess we must resort back to our initial tactics." His breath was hot against my skin. "You realize I hate being on the phone."

"Me too, but I hate being away from you even more." I confessed.

"I cannot believe how attached I've become to you in such a short time." My heart leaped in my chest. "It feels like we've been together forever, but in a good way."

"I know what you mean." I pulled his arms tighter around me. "I feel the same way. It's hard to imagine my life without you."

"Is this crazy?"

"Yes. Completely." I rolled over to face him. "I always laughed at people who said it was love at first sight, but I'm not laughing anymore." I leaned over and kissed his nose in a sweet, playful manner. "I mean, not exactly love at first sight, but a couple of days rather." I giggled.

"When did you know?" His piercing blue eyes sparkled.

"That I loved you?"

"Uh huh."

"When you showed up at my door to help me with my research and presentation. That was the sweetest gesture you could have made." I smiled. "And when you ordered dinners for Brylee and the ice cream, that just showed me what a kind and compassionate man you are."

"So, I fooled you completely." His devilish smile widened.

"Yes. You did."

"I knew I loved you the first time we spoke. You started cussing about the police and people's driving skills. It was hilarious. I realized you were the perfect woman for me. I used to think I was bad, but I don't hold a candle to you." He teased.

"Bull shit." I shoved him away playfully.

"You're adorable. But you're vicious when it comes to driving."

"Stupid people irritate me." I admitted. "People down here don't seem to understand the concept of 'lane ending' or what that little stick on the side of their steering wheel is used for."

"Angry driver." He mocked.

"I am not." I staunchly defended myself. "I simply have an intolerance for morons." I explained.

"I love you, Arya." Deuce smiled. "Your little quirks are charming. Your OCD tendencies are amusing."

"OCD?" I raised my eyebrows at him.

"Your closet is organized by style and color-coded. The volume on the TV and radio have to be on an even number." He giggled. "You obsessively clean when you get nervous or upset. And I love how you have to fold the towels a specific way, and if I try to help you fold laundry, you go behind me and refold it when you think I'm not looking. And I love using them to screw with you."

"You're mean." I couldn't believe how observant he was. One of the joys of dating a law enforcement officer as I was learning.

"You only say that when I point out the truth and you don't like it." Deuce laughed even harder.

"Do not." But we both knew it was true.

"I think it's cute."

"I don't." I childishly stuck out my tongue at him. "You enjoy being a pain in my ass."

"I thought you enjoyed it." He reached over and started tickling me.

"Stop it!" I squealed, twisting, and turning, trying to fight away from him.

"You love it." He laughed and continued his torment.

"No! No!" I thrust about my bed. "Please! Please! Stop it!"

"Truce?" He pinned me down.

"Truce." I struggled to catch my breath.

Deuce leaned down and kissed me passionately. The stubble on his face grazed against my skin, but I didn't care. I wanted to savor every moment with him and devour him in the process.

I ran my hands over his back, letting the warmth of his skin seep into my fingertips. The feel of his body hovering over mine, the slight weight of him on me held my body to the earth.

His lips traveled down my neck to my shoulder. His breath was hot, his breathing heavy. His hand slowly began to massage my breasts as he brought his lips down to it. He suckled on it intensely as if there was no tomorrow.

I nudged him over and rolled over on top of him. I kissed him overpoweringly, locking our hands together over his head. I paused and looked down at him. The dim lights made his eyes sparkle and cast warm hues over his face and body. He had never looked so sexy.

I maneuvered my way over his throbbing, thick, cock and slid slowly down upon it. It felt glorious, filling me up completely. I loved his cock and the way he used it. He was such an incredible lover.

I leaned back with our hands still locked together and moaned loudly. Deuce moved his hips in perfect rhythm with mine. He held me up as our momentum increased, leaving us both grasping and wanting more. I could never get enough of him and could never tire of making love to him.

I let go of his hands and dug my nails into his chest, trying to balance myself as ecstasy ripped through my body. Deuce arched himself into me and moaned loudly. His hold on my hips was almost painful but didn't fully register in my euphoria.

I collapsed upon his chest, wholly spent in my joyful bliss.

Our breathing was labored; our bodies sweaty and spent. But I didn't want to move. I wanted to hold onto this moment, this man. I knew I was only going to be gone for a short while, but in this moment, it felt like an eternity.

FIFTEEN

BRYLEE AND I HIT THE ROAD the next evening a little after eight. I found through trial and error that it was best to travel at night. The drive through Los Angeles was easiest to manage in the wee hours of the morning. The first five hours of the journey was a long and arduous trek through the desert. It was the worse part of the trip.

We ran into an unusual thunderstorm about an hour outside of Phoenix, and it rained all the way to Palm Springs. The roads in the desert weren't like the ones in the Midwest that are equipped to handle heavy downpour. Rather than running off to the sides, water simply stands causing travel to slow down to a crawl.

What should have taken us five hours, quickly turned into nine. We crept into LA already exhausted and cranky. Traffic was picking up, and everything I had driven all night to avoid was now surrounding me. We passed through the city and started climbing into the grapevine. We'd barely passed through the bypass when we got rerouted.

I pulled into a gas station to fuel up, stretch, eat, and use the restroom. My entire body was aching, and all I wanted to do was sleep. The station was packed with people getting kicked off the interstate. Our brief stop took us almost an hour. The station attendant informed me that the pass through the grapevine was closed due to mudslides.

I pulled off to the side of the road and tried to reset my GPS to find an alternative route. But for some reason, my phone would not update. I knew the coastal highway would take me up to Fresno or San Francisco, but I couldn't locate a route to take me over there.

I finally gave up. Between the frustration and fatigue, I was at my wit's end. I called Deuce and asked for his help.

"Hey, what's going on?" His voice was light and cheerful.

"The grapevine is closed because of some mudslides. My phone won't reroute us. Can you help please?" I was almost in tears.

"You sound exhausted." He chuckled.

"We hit that storm on our way to LA." I stated. "It's taken us twice as long as it normally does."

"I'm sorry. Are you okay?"

"No. Can you help me, please?" I begged him.

"What do you need?"

"Help getting over to the 101 from the 5."

"All right. Let me pull up maps."

Deuce got us over to the 101 and talked to me up the coastline trying to keep me awake. He was so incredible. It gave Brylee a chance to doze off for a bit since she didn't have to play navigator. She had been nodding off for the last hour.

He stirred us through the bypass to Fresno back over to the 99. We were cruising along at 75 to 80, trying to make some time. Brylee was snoring quietly beside me. I was happy that at least one of us was able to get some sleep. I was excited about her taking over when she woke up.

"Oh, my God!" The car jolted and pulled to the right abruptly.

"What's wrong?" Deuce pipped up.

"I don't know." I pulled off to the shoulder.

I put on my hazard lights and sighed heavily. We had been on the road for almost fifteen hours. I had been driving the entire time and couldn't take much more. I opened my door and walked around the car. The front passenger tire was shredded. We weren't going anywhere, anytime soon.

"I give." I leaned against the hood. "This is a sign. I'm coming home."

"What happened?"

"The front tire on the passenger side is gone. There's nothing but the rim." I ran my fingers through my hair.

"Okay. It's all right. Do you have AAA?" He asked.

"No. But I have roadside assistance through my insurance." I told him.

"Give them a call and call me back. It's gonna be fine. You've been waiting since Christmas to see your son and grandson. You can't turn back now." Deuce comforted me.

"I know. I know." I got back in my car. "I'll call you back."

After our layover at Discount Tires in Fresno, three hours later Brylee and I were back on the road. By the time we reached the cabin at Lake Tahoe, we had been on the road for eighteen hours. I wasn't sure if I was ready to laugh or cry. I got out of the car and collapsed into my son's arms.

~

Carson was standing in the driveway when we arrived. He was pulling the pack 'n play out of the back of Alicia's car. He smiled and waved as we pulled up.

I barely got the car in park and shut off before I leaped out of the car and into his arms. It felt like forever since I'd last held my son. I missed him so much it made my heart ache.

"Hey momma," my son laughed as I almost knocked him off his feet.

Carson's six-foot-three solid broad frame towered over me. He had grown into a strikingly handsome man with his sandy blond hair and hazel-green eyes. The slim young man I had placed on a bus eight short years ago had been completely transformed courtesy of the US Army.

"I missed you." I rested my head against his chest and squeezed him tightly.

"I missed you, too." He squeezed me tightly before finally releasing me. "I was beginning to get worried. We were expecting you for breakfast, noon at the latest."

"It was a rough trip. I'm just glad we're here."

"Go on inside. I'll get the bags." I handed him the keys and watched as Brylee came around and hugged her brother. It warmed my heart, seeing the two of them together again.

"Hey mom," Alicia came out onto the porch holding my beautiful grandson.

"Hi, darling." I walked up and gave them a hug. "When did you get here?"

"Last night at about eight. Sawyer was so cranky we just stuck him in bed with us. He didn't mind flying, but the time difference is starting to wear on him." She explained.

"Ah, come to grandma little man." I lifted him out of her arms and hugged him tightly kissing the top of his head. "I missed you."

"He's missed you, too."

"He's gotten so big." I complained following her and Brylee into the cabin.

Our little hideaway for the next week was nestled in Boiler's Point between Tahoe Vista and Kings Beach. Although it was waterfront property, it was surrounded by gorgeously dense woods. The large covered front porch held a couple rockers and a table and chairs.

The steps lead down to a vast lawn leading off to a long pier with comfortable oversized patio furniture. The views were breathtaking and more picturesque than imaginable. It was our second time renting the cabin, and it was my favorite little getaway from the hectic lifestyle I lived in Phoenix.

Carson put my bags in my room and joined the rest of us in the living room. He had started a fire taking the chill out of the evening air. I listened to them recall their journey from Fort Campbell and how delightful it was going through airport security with an infant and all their luggage and baby gear.

Alicia noticed me nodding in and out with Sawyer sleeping in my arms. "Here, mom, let me take him. You're exhausted."

"Thanks, hon." I stood up and wobbled a little. Carson reached out and grabbed my arm to steady me. "Thanks." I grinned wearily. "I think I'm going to take a hot shower and head to bed." I gave them all hugs and kisses and drudged my tired bones back to my room.

~

I came downstairs in the morning with the smell of fresh coffee and bacon in the air. My stomach growled with anticipation. I walked into the kitchen, finding Sawyer squealing happily and shoving Cheerio's in mouth.

"Good morning, little man. How's grandma's favorite guy?" I leaned over and kissed him on top of his head." Sawyer screeched and tried to hand me some of his cereal. "Thank you." I pretended to eat them, making my grandson clap with joy.

"Good morning," I said to Carson and Alicia as I tossed them into the sink on my way to the coffee maker.

"Morning," their sleepy voices replied. "How did you sleep?" Carson asked.

"Like the dead." I poured my coffee and sat down beside him at the table. "I'm still exhausted. That ride was a nightmare."

"I'm just glad you made it here safely." Alicia set down a plate piled high with pancakes and another with bacon. "Eat up, everyone."

We hardly put a dent in our first helpings before Brylee came bouncing into the room. She looked refreshed; her hair still wet from her morning shower. She promptly grabbed some coffee and sat down with us.

"Good morning, people. I'm starved." She started piling up her plate while the rest of us stared at her, trying not to giggle.

"How did you sleep?" Alicia inquired.

"Alone." She rolled her eyes. "Splendidly."

"Good." I smiled at her.

"Sometimes it sucks being the only one that's single." She huffed.

"Momma's single. She just got the master because she's paying." Carson giggled.

"Momma's not single, big bro. She's got a hot little police officer in her back pocket." Brylee mocked.

"He is not in my back pocket." I gave her a disapproving look. "When you say something like that, it sounds really bad. If the wrong person overheard you, they could easily misunderstand your meaning."

"Seriously, momma? Relax. It's just us, and I was teasing." She flipped her wet hair to the side and rolled her eyes. "Besides, the way you drive it couldn't hurt." She teased.

"Are you bad-mouthing my driving?" I asked.

"If you got a ticket every time you got pulled over, you wouldn't even have a license." She reminded me.

"I've gotten much better." I defended myself. "I've stopped tail-gating." I snorted.

"You add ten or twenty and 'ish' after every speed limit sign." My son teased.

"I do not." I stated although I knew it was true.

"Yes, you do." The three answered in unison and busted out laughing.

"Whatever." I rolled my eyes at them with a coy smile.

"I think it's great you're dating someone?" Alicia's gaze landed directly on me.

"Sort of, yeah, I umm ..." I wasn't sure what to say to my son.

"Sort of?" Brylee scoffed. "He's practically living with us." Brylee announced.

"Is this true, momma?" Carson turned towards me.

"Yes, it's true." I'm not sure why I was so hesitant to tell him.

"Who is he? I'm guessing he's a cop?" My son wrinkled his nose. "Seriously, momma? A cop? Why? They're all assholes."

"He's a homicide detective for the Phoenix PD. And he's not an asshole. I wouldn't be dating him if he was." I assured him.

"All cops are lying assholes, momma. You know that." He huffed.

I knew Carson's experience with the police back home when he was in high school was nothing but negative. I had expected this reaction from him and had dreaded telling him about Deuce.

"Honestly, he's not like that." I looked over at Brylee. "Tell him."

"It's true." She admitted. "I actually like him a lot. He's really sweet and treats mom great. You would like him." She took another bite of her pancake.

"How long have you been seeing him?" Caron inquired.

"About a month." I admitted.

"And he's already living with you? Come on, momma. I know it's hard being on your own, but why?"

"Okay, I've got to say something here. First, our mother gets asked out a lot and turns down men all the time. If she ever does have dinner with them, only two have gotten a second date in the last year, and this cop is one of them." She smiled over at me. "Secondly, he truly does care a lot about momma. And finally, he makes her happy. I've never seen her smile so much. They really are cute together."

"What's his name?" Alicia inquired.

"Grayson Steglich, but everyone calls him Deuce." I said.

"Deuce?" Carson looked confused. "Why, Deuce?"

"Apparently, all cops have nicknames, and his is after some guy from ESPN or something. I don't know. Something about football." I shrugged.

"You mean Duce Staley? The former running back with the Eagles?" My son was a football encyclopedia.

"I guess so."

"Is he an Eagles fan?" He asked.

"I don't know. You'd have to ask him." I was clueless.

"Okay." Carson shrugged. "When do I get to meet him?"

"Like I said, it's only been a month. We'll see what happens." I casually took a bite of my bacon and downplay the seriousness of our relationship.

"Brylee has met him." Carson added.

"Brylee lives with me. You live at Fort Campbell. Big difference." I smirked and shook my head at him.

"Geographical technicality." My son could be such a smart-ass.

"But a big one." I pointed out.

"As long as you're happy, that's all that's important." Alicia gave her husband a look that silenced him. I had to look down at my plate so he wouldn't see me smiling.

SIXTEEN

THE FOURTH OF JULY DAWNED bright and cloudless. The sun was glistening off the water. I poured myself an over-sized mug of coffee and strolled down to the pier in my pajamas with a light blanket draped around my shoulders. The sun had barely broken the horizon, and the colors were bouncing off the water like diamonds.

I snuggled into one of the patio couches and curled my feet beneath me. The air had a bit of a chill in it, and my body was so acclimated to the Phoenix heat that anything below eighty degrees felt like Midwest winter.

My family was still sleeping peacefully. I sipped my coffee and rested my head against the cushions. It was hard to imagine how much my life had changed in the last four years. I was so grateful for the long and adventurous journey that had allowed my firm to flourish and brought Deuce into my life.

~

Brylee, Alicia, and Carson left after breakfast to go Kayaking.

I agreed to stay home and spend some time spoiling Sawyer. I wanted to spend as much time as possible with him before they headed back to Tennessee.

I took Sawyer for a walk in his stroller to the small craft fair and farmer's market being held by local artists and grocers. I picked up some fresh fruit and greens for a spinach salad for dinner. I was planning on having a barbeque on the grill complete with Caron's favorite homemade potato salad, deviled eggs, and baked beans.

I was having such a great time with my grandson. I felt like I was twenty years old again and pushing his father around. He reminded me so much of his dad. The resemblance between them was uncanny. Sawyer had a smile and laugh that could brighten any room, and it wasn't long before strangers were saying hello and remarking on how handsome and sweet he was.

After I put the groceries away, I fed Sawyer his lunch. He had a wonderful time playing with his food, and it wasn't long before he needed a bath. I let him splash in the bubbles while I tried to get the food out of his fine hair.

Sawyer squirmed about as I tried to dress him. I had forgotten how much fun dressing an eleven-month old could be. I tickled him and sang nursery rhymes to him making him laugh so I could put his new Fourth of July outfit on him.

I carried him out onto the porch and sat down in one of the rockers. Sawyer was rubbing his eyes and getting a bit fussy. I rocked him gently and nestled him close to me. He closed his eyes and made the cutest little suckling noises as he drifted off to sleep. I couldn't bring myself to carry him inside and put him in the pack 'n play.

The rest of my household returned in the late afternoon. I was still on the porch rocking Sawyer enjoying the sounds of his cooing, the birds singing in the surrounding woods, and the laughter of racing around on the boats drinking and skiing the holiday away.

Sawyer stirred at the sound of his parent's voices and began to cry. Alicia lifted him from my lap and carried him inside.

"How long have you been out here?" Carson asked, carrying a case of beer.

"What time is it?" I stood up and stretched my aching back and legs.

"Almost four." He held open the door for his sister and me.

"About four hours." I responded.

"You held him his entire nap?" He chuckled. "Yeah, we're not going to pay for that one."

"Oh, hush. It's my right as grandma." I childishly stuck my tongue out at my son.

Carson manned the grill while the girls and I fixed the rest of dinner together. The kids were enjoying the beer, and I had cracked open a bottle of peach white wine. Brylee had turned on some music and Sawyer was scooting around the kitchen in his walker bumping into everyone's ankles.

By the time we sat down to eat, everyone was in good spirits. Carson was easily on his sixth beer, and the girls had just opened their second. I knew Carson had started drinking heavily in the military, especially after his deployments. Recently, thanks to Alicia, he had given up the whiskey and was now drinking beer.

"Hey momma, what are your plans for after the fireworks?" Carson was heaping the potato salad on his plate.

"I don't know. I hadn't thought about it." I answered.

"Well, while we were out today, we heard about this rooftop party across the lake." He stated casually.

"And you three would like to go check it out?" I chuckled. "Ah, to be young again."

"You are young, momma." Brylee smiled.

"I'm not in my twenties." I smiled. "You three go and have fun. I'm happy to stay here with Sawyer."

"He'll be asleep before we leave." Alicia pipped up.

"Don't worry. We'll be fine." I assured her. "You guys have fun. And don't drink and drive."

"Spoken like a true parent." Carson teased.

"We aren't kids anymore." Brylee reminded me.

"I am aware, but you're still my kids, and it doesn't matter how old you get; I still worry about you."

~

We made our way down to the pier as twilight fell over the clear waters. Alicia curled up to Carson with their feet dangling in the water. Brylee was still wearing her red and white striped bikini top with the red bottoms. She had thrown on a pair of jean shorts with them, and her red flip flops. She had pulled her long hair up into a messy bun, and her make up was applied sparingly. She looked adorable.

The lake was filled with boats of every size and shape. Some of the families in the pontoons were barbequing, and it seemed the speedboaters were consuming more alcohol and a lot rowdier. The lake appeared to be on fire with the number of sparklers. They were enhanced by the sporadic fireworks that tore through the black sky.

I sat down in one of the oversized chairs with Sawyer on my lap. He was wide awake and wasn't interested in sitting still. He didn't flinch when a firework exploded overhead but seemed rather oblivious to it. He squirmed and fought until Carson turned around and took him from me.

I watched as my son took his little mini-me and set him between his legs. Sawyer squealed in delight as Carson held him back with one arm but allowed his feet to splash in the water. I leaned back against the cushions pulling my sweater tighter around me.

The chilly northern California breeze fell upon us bringing goosebumps across my arms and legs. I closed my eyes for a moment and wished that Deuce was sitting here beside me with his arm around me and the heat from his body warming mine. I missed him so much. I had only been away from him for a few days, but it felt so much longer.

The fireworks show started, and the sky was ablaze with color. From our pier, we had a picturesque view. I took a sip of my wine and relaxed. It was as if the heat from the fireworks had taken the chill out of the air, and it was suddenly comforting. Sawyer calmed down, and soon after the show began, he was sound asleep in his mother's arms.

SEVENTEEN

THURSDAY AFTERNOON WAS GORGEOUS. The sky was a bright blue scattered with white fluffy clouds. The temperature hovered in the mid-eighties, and for someone who had been roasting in the triple digits, it felt a bit chilly. The backyard of the cabin was filled with trees, a cobblestone walkway leading to a little koi pond.

I walked off the deck with an old blanket, a copy of John Jakes' *Love and War*, the baby monitor, an iced coffee, and my cell. I found a large shade tree and spread it out under it. The grass was thick and lush. Ever since I'd moved to Phoenix, it was the one thing I missed more than anything — green.

I dearly missed walking barefoot in the grass, large birch, and maple trees, and towering pine trees. I longed for the days of sitting on the back porch swing with a good book and feeling the summer breeze filled with the smell of fresh cut grass engulfing me. I missed my blossoming flower beds, pulling the weeds in the early morning hours when the grass was still blanketed in dew.

But those days were gone now; lost to a past that was nothing more than a painful blur of a time almost forgotten. And there was no point in looking back. While I dearly cherished the memories of my children's youth, I also hated that it was consumed with such emotional turmoil. It was the darkest period of my life.

I sat down and kick off my sandals. I dug my toes into the grass and laid back on the blanket. The sunlight was sparkling through the leaves, causing its traces to look like fireflies twinkling in a mid-summer twilight. I closed my eyes and stretched out listening to the birds calling to each other.

I rolled over upon my stomach and picked up my book. I was only on the third chapter. I absolutely loved the first book in the series, North and South, and as soon as I had finished it, I rushed out to purchase a copy of the second. Unfortunately, between my budding relationship with Deuce and work, I had very little free time to read lately.

I made it to chapter five when my phone rang. A smile spread across my face as I saw Deuce's picture on my screen.

"Hello, darling. How are you?"

"Good. How are things going? Are you having fun?"

"Yes. I'm loving it. Sawyer just went down for his nap, so I snuck outside to read. Brylee is off somewhere doing God only knows what. Carson and Alicia went to the store, so I'm lounging in the backyard under the trees with a book and the baby monitor. It's gorgeous out today. I miss this." I told him.

"I'm glad you're relaxing. It's about time." He chuckled.

"How is your day going?"

"I'm on-call, so I can't really do anything. Munchkin is at her mom's, and my mom went out to lunch with her friends. I'm just sitting around here, cleaning up the house and missing you."

"Sounds exciting."

"Very." He huffed. "It's so strange not seeing you every day."

"I know. I miss you so much." I rested my head on my arm and closed my eyes, picturing Deuce's smile.

"I miss you too."

"How are the kids? Are you enjoying being a grandma?" He teased.

"I love it. Sawyer is the cutest little man. He looks exactly like Carson when he was that age. I swear they are twins. I can't get enough of him. I feel like I miss everything with him." I complained.

"I'm still trying to get over the fact that you're a grandma." He snickered. "My daughter isn't even ten yet."

"I'm only a year older than you. I simply started early." I reminded him.

"It's hard for me to imagine having grown children; especially grandchildren. I'm dreading Madelyn hitting the double digits."

"Trust me, it goes so fast. One day you're dropping them off at kindergarten, and the next day they are in a graduation gown, and you're standing there wondering what the hell happened."

"So, I've been told." He scoffed.

"I know you don't believe me, but it's true. I remember thinking I had all the time in the world to do things with my kids and then one day I was dropping Carson off at the station that would take him to boot camp. I remember going home and sitting on his bed, crying for hours. I couldn't believe he was gone. Despite all the fighting we did during his teen years, I hated the thought of him not being there. The house felt empty. Lonely." Tears escaped out of the corners of my eyes.

"I've got a while before that happens." Deuce stated.

"When Carson was in high school, he was always in trouble; drinking, partying, never opened a book, caused chaos in every class. I swear his principal had me on speed dial. There were days when I couldn't wait for him to graduate and move out just so I could have some peace and quiet in my life. Now, I'd give anything to have him little again. Brylee too."

"Carson's a boy. All boys get into mischief, and it doesn't

necessarily end at graduation or boot camp. I've managed to do more stupid shit since I joined the department than I ever did in high school."

"Oh, really. Such as?" It was hard to imagine.

"If I tell you, you can't laugh." I could hear the smile on his voice.

"You know I can't promise you that." I chuckled.

"Fair enough. Okay, well, one time about years after I joined the department, I was called to a shelter downtown for a stabbing. A transient had stabbed another one. The victim said that there was two of them, both Hispanic and they had taken off on a bike. A few miles away, I came across this large Hispanic man on a bike. He was so large at first, I didn't see the little guy in front of him on the bike. When I realized it, I jumped out of my car so fast I didn't get it completely into park. The little guy pulled his knife on me, so I had to draw my weapon." He started laughing despite himself.

"So, I'm standing there holding this guy at gunpoint and out of the corner of my eye I notice my car rolling down the hill. Then I see Gina, my superior, flying past me and swerving in front of my car to keep it from hitting any one of the cars parked along the side of the street. I hear that loud 'boom' and realize my car had just plowed into the driver's side door of her car. She couldn't open the door, and all I hear is her voice; "God damn it, Deuce!"

"Oh, my God! You jumped out of the car without putting it in park?" I hooted. "That's fabulous!"

"Oh, shut up." I could picture the look on his sweet face, his eyes sparkling with deviousness. "One time, I was chasing a suspect on foot, and he ran through a yard. So, I followed him, and suddenly, I felt a sharp pain across my thighs. Apparently, I'd run through a part of the yard that had a low-level fence, and I'd hit it about three inches below my crotch."

"Thankfully." I added.

"Yes, thankfully. The next day I had a huge bruise across my thighs. I could hardly walk."

"I guess when you ran track in high school, hurdles weren't a part of that." I couldn't resist teasing him.

"It was dark. I couldn't see anything." He argued.

"Don't you carry a flashlight?" I was having fun.

"You have no idea what it's like when you're chasing an armed suspect and your adrenaline kicks in." He informed me.

"You're right, I don't. I can't imagine living in your world." I admitted.

"Those occasions are rare. But we are close and do razz each other worse than any siblings ever could. The guys in my unit are ruthless. And I'm not being sexist. By guys, I mean both men and women."

"How politically correct of you." I snorted.

"Thank you." Deuce mocked. "One time, a few years back. I drove a full-size truck instead of the city car I have now. I was coming off a triple homicide and had been up for almost thirty hours. I was dead on my feet and struggling to keep my eyes open. I parked in one of the bays at the garage, logged in some evidence, and when I pulled out, I soon realized I hadn't shut the passenger door. The door, in the process of being bent backward, also took out the bay stall wall." I laughed. "Now, whenever anyone in my unit parks there, they take a picture of it and text it to me."

"I'm sorry, but that's funny." I giggled.

"No, it's not. It's been three years, and the city still hasn't fixed that damn wall yet." He complained.

"I can understand why they give you so much shit."

"Fuck you." He smirked.

"You only say that when you know, I'm right." I kept laughing.

"You're so mean." He told me.

"Hey darling, my son and Alicia just got back. I'm going to go help them get things ready for dinner." I heard a car door shut and their voices over the breeze.

"Fine. Be that way." He teased. "Have fun with your family. Call me before you go to bed."

"I will." I promised.

"I love you."

"I love you, too."

I picked up my things and carried them back into the house. Carson and Alicia were unloading grocery bags and putting things away. I jumped right in and started helping.

"Is Sawyer still sleeping?" My daughter-in-law asked.

"Not a peep." I smiled. "Sleeping like an angel."

"That's the only time he's an angel." Alicia snickered.

"Yeah, he's got a lot of Carson in him and not just his looks." I told her.

"He's a carbon copy of Carson. There's not a trace of me in that kid." She gave Carson a playful shove as she passed him on her way to the fridge.

"It's not my fault my genes are stronger than yours." He taunted.

"Did you get any reading done?" Alicia asked.

"Not really. Deuce called shortly after you guys left." I said casually.

"It's all right if you like this guy, momma." Carson told me.

"I know, baby. It's just strange talking to you about someone else." I confessed.

"Umm, you do know dad is seeing someone else, too. Right?"

"I'm not surprised." I muttered.

"I guess you know her." He said in a low voice. "Apparently, you went to school with her — Kari Kaplin." Carson stated.

"I heard." I snorted.

"I'm guessing you do know her." Alicia observed.

"Yeah. She graduated a year before my sister. Her sister was in my class. She's a hot mess according to her parents. They went to our church back home. Her mom was my Girl Scout leader when I was in elementary school. She told me years ago that Kari was heavily into drugs and had lost custody of her three kids — that she has with three different men." I rolled my eyes.

"Wow." Alicia said in a low voice.

"Yeah. She's a winner. She's been in and out of rehab for years from what my friend, Aaron, told me last Christmas. I guess she was homeless, and that's how she ended up living with your dad." I said.

"She's made some bad decisions." Carson agreed. 'Dad said she's trying to put her life back together."

"Well, you know I honestly could care less about her pathetic and sad little life or what's she's gone through, because everything she's done, she's done to herself. What pisses me off about her being involved with your dad is...you remember Max? Our favorite dog that my grandfather gave you when you were four." I turned towards my son.

"Of course. She was my baby."

"Well, that bitch was working as a vet assistant at our vet's office when we were forced to put her down. It was one of the few sober periods in her adult life. She was the one who put the needle in Max's paw and then had the audacity to comfort me. I was distraught. That dog was family. She was my baby." I brushed the tears off my face. "And I found out later that she was seducing my husband. How's that for someone with high moral standing?" I scoffed. "They deserve each other." I put down the cheese and walked out onto the back porch.

A few minutes later, Alicia joined me on the swing. The sun was setting over the clear waters, and the evening air was moving in, and the temperature was dropping. I hastily brushed the tears off my cheeks and wrapped my arms around myself.

"Are you okay?" She asked.

Alicia had joined our family long before she married my son. They went to school together and had become close friends during high school. She was one of his closest friends, and I knew they liked each other. She was always around our home, and I loved her. She was a calming influence on my son.

He was also too wild for her to date during high school. They got together shortly after graduation and then eloped during his first year in the military. I wasn't upset in his choice of a spouse because I loved Alicia like another daughter. I was devastated that they had eloped, and I missed seeing my only son get married. I was furious when I found out and reacted very badly.

"I hope you don't think this is about Todd or Kari." I gave her a weak smile.

"I know, it's not."

"It's ..." my voice trailed off.

"Max." She said in a low voice.

"I know it sounds silly. But we had her for twelve years, and she slept on the floor beside me every night. She protected the kids. She used to walk them down to the bus stop every morning and then wait in the front yard until three. Then she'd go down there and wait for the bus to drop her kids off so she could walk them home." I sighed heavily. "And she would lay in the neighbors front yard across the street when the kids were shootin' hoops so she could guard the parameter around them." I brushed more tears away. "And that bitch tarnished my last memory of her. I hate her for that."

"She can't change all those years of memories you have of Max." Alicia assured me.

"I know. It just irks me."

"I could show you something that will make you laugh." A sly grin spread across her lips as she shifted in the swing, getting more comfortable. She retrieved her phone from her back pocket and began scrolling. "You remember how vain Todd always was?"

"That's putting it nicely." I scoffed. "He spent more on his hair stylist and products than me." I rolled my eyes.

"I remember his working out in that home gym he put in his man cave." Alicia had the most devious look in her eyes. "I guess he's given that up." She handed me her phone.

On the screen, she had pulled up Todd's profile on her Facebook page. There was a picture of him taken three weeks ago. He resembled nothing of the man I'd walked out on over four years ago. There was no trace of the man I'd spend most of my adult life with.

The man on the tiny screen had more than a five o'clock shadow on his chubby face, and his hair was shaggy and unkempt. I was utterly astounded. I couldn't think of anything to say. I simply stared at the photo, not knowing who the man in the photo was.

"His company transferred him to Colorado last year. It looks like they are both taking full advantage of the legalization of marijuana." Alicia laughed wholeheartedly.

"It certainly seems so." I was still too stunned to laugh.

"I was shocked when I saw it on my newsfeed. I showed it to Carson, and he wasn't surprised at all. It seems instead of him helping Kari straighten her life out, she's ruined his. He's such a mess that Carson won't speak to him. I haven't either. The last time we saw him before they moved, he was nothing like the man he used to be."

"This is the same man who tortured and ridiculed me for gaining five pounds after I had shoulder surgery and couldn't work out?"

"I know." She shook her head in disbelief. "I find it ironic. He bitched about your size fives being tight, and then he lets himself fall apart."

"What does Carson say about it?"

"Not much. He doesn't bring him up. He was upset when he showed up at the hospital when Sawyer was born, especially since he was stuck at Fort Benning for training." She said. "I wanted to send him away, but I didn't want to start a family fight."

"I wouldn't have been upset." I snorted.

"Does Brylee talk to him?"

"Not in the last several years." I looked down at my hands. "The things he said and did, not just to me, but to her; I don't know if she'll ever forgive him." I said.

"I understand. My relationship with my dad is rocky on the best of days." Alicia chuckled.

"I'm sorry. I wish I could fix everything for all three of you, but you're all adults now, and I have to take a step back." I put my hand on hers. "I can't say I like it much." I smiled, warmly at her.

"It's funny how much your perspective changes after you have a child of your own. I used to hate it how my mother hovered over me, and now that I have Sawyer, I'd do anything to keep him safe."

"Welcome to motherhood. I'm happy to say that you're very good at it."

"I try. I still have a lot to learn." She sighed with a smile."

"Sweetheart, I'm still learning." I leaned over and embraced her. "Come on. Let's get dinner started."

Brylee had returned home and was playing on the floor with Sawyer when we walked back in the cabin. Carson was lounging in the recliner playing Mortal Combat on the X-box One. I smiled at my family. They were all healthy and happy. And despite all that they had gone through with the divorce, they had survived. I could not have been more at peace with the world.

~

My son and his family were heading out first thing in the morning. Their flight was scheduled to leave at nine, and they had a good hour drive to the airport.

I leaned against the railing holding Sawyer in my arms while Carson loaded up their rental car and Alicia double-checked to make sure they didn't leave anything behind. I kissed Sawyer's chubby little cherub face leaving traces of my tears on his cheeks.

This was the dreaded part of my trip. I hated saying goodbye to my family. Carson and I had always been so close, and despite his age and the uniform he wore proudly, he was still my baby boy. I swayed Sawyer back and forth and hummed; You are my Sunshine. It was Carson's song.

"And I thought I was your sunshine, momma." My son kissed me quickly on the cheek as he passed by me on his way back into the cabin.

"Always, my darling." My heart was ripping in two.

"You need to give him his own song." Carson hollered over his shoulder.

"Yes, I can do that, little man." I looked down at my grandson and kissed him again.

The car was loaded, and Carson and Alicia stood beside it. This was the moment I dreaded. Letting them go was so difficult. I squeezed Sawyer tightly and told him once more how much grandma loves him. I kissed him one last time and handed him to Alicia. Sawyer was jabbering away, and all smiles as she turned to buckle him in his car seat. Brylee quickly hugged and kissed her brother. As soon as she released him, I reached out and grabbed my son.

"Please be careful. Text when you reach the airport and then call me once you land." I held him tightly with tears pouring down my face. "I love you so much." I touched the side of his face. "I miss you every day."

"I miss you too, momma." Carson gave me a kiss. "I love you. And I promise we'll see you soon." All I could do was nod as I let him go.

"Don't worry, mom." Alicia came around and wrapped her arms around me. "I'll take care of them."

"I know you will, sweetheart." I kissed her on the cheek and then looked at her beautiful face. "They are the most important men in my life, and I trust you with them. I love you."

"I love you, too." She smiled. "I'll call you when we get home."

I stood in the driveway holding Brylee's hand watching my son and his family drive down the lane and around the corner. I brushed the tears off my cheeks. The hardest part of parenthood is letting your child do exactly what you always dreamed they'd become; strong, independent, loving, successful adults.

EIGHTEEN

I CALLED DEUCE AS I PULLED onto 99 South. It was eleven in the morning, and the sun was already baking overhead. The cloudless sky told me it was going to be a hot day, and I knew the temperatures were only going to get worse the closer I got to Phoenix.

I dreaded making the ride solo. I'd done it before last Christmas when Brylee had flown out to visit her dad's parents for a couple days and was going to meet up with us at Lake Tahoe. I had sung along with Christmas carols the entire way and taken my time. I was surprised at how relaxing the trip had been. Nothing like the disastrous trip this time around.

"Hello darling, how is your morning going?" I asked.

"I'm still at the office. Are you on the road yet?"

"I'm on the ninety-nine heading home." I informed him.

"Okay. Well, let me call you when I leave the office. I'll be getting outta here around one."

"All right." I was a bit bummed he couldn't talk.

"Be careful."

"I will."

"Love you."

"I love you, too."

I turned up the radio to Queen and rolled the windows down. The California breeze blew through the car like a welcomed old friend. My hair flew around my face, and I kept trying to tuck it behind my ears. I finally gave up and grabbed a clip out of my purse; steadied the car with my knee and twisted my hair up.

I loved this time of year. I hated leaving my kids and Sawyer, but it had felt so good to have some time alone without anything weighing on my shoulders. I knew I had a lot of work waiting for me when I returned, but I didn't want to think about that now.

At this moment, it was just me, Queen, and the open road before me.

~

My cell phone lost its signal and dropped my call with Deuce as I climbed into the mountain pass. We had been talking for more than three hours. He enjoyed listening to my battle with the LA traffic and panic moments fighting my way across six lanes of traffic to switch from one interstate to the next. This was the dreaded point of the journey.

I was struggling to stay awake and missing Brylee's endless chatter. I rolled down the window and let the cool desert breeze flow through the car. I tuned in my satellite radio into an 80s hair band channel and turned the volume up to a deafening rate.

I was finally able to reach Deuce again three hours later about an hour outside of Phoenix. It was almost eleven o'clock, and I pulled over to get some gas and coffee.

"Hello, darling." His sleepy voice rang through my speakers.

"Hi, baby." I'd never been so happy to hear his voice. "Did I wake you?"

"Yeah." He grumbled.

"I'm sorry."

"It's okay. Where are you?" He asked.

"About an hour outside of Phoenix."

"That's good." He yawned loudly. "I'm exhausted. Call me when you get home?"

"Umm, okay." I gritted my teeth together with fury.

"Be careful." He muttered. "I love you." Then he was gone before I could even respond.

"Damn you!" I spat and tossed my phone into the passenger seat.

I pulled out of the gas station and back onto the interstate, fuming. I took a sip of my coffee and struggled to keep my eyes open and focused on the road before me. I was counting on Deuce talking to me to keep me awake on the final leg of my journey. But apparently, he cared more about his precious sleep.

I reached out and grabbed my phone. I hated calling Shelly this late at night, but I was desperate. I'd rather interrupt her sleep than fall asleep myself and have an accident.

"Hey, girl. How are you? Where are you?" Her voice was bright and cheerful — such a welcomed reprieve.

"Dead. About an hour outside of Phoenix."

"You sound dead."

"I feel it. I'm struggling. I need you to keep me awake." I told her.

"I'm surprised you didn't call Deuce."

"The asshole would rather sleep than talk to me." I said in a shitty tone.

"Did he work today?"

"Yes."

"Call-out?"

"Not today, but he had three this week." I explained.

"So, he probably is exhausted."

"I know." I realized how selfish I sounded.

"Then you should probably let him sleep."

"Which is why I'm calling you." I countered

"But you sound irritated." She noted.

"I am, I guess."

"Why?"

"Because I've been looking forward to seeing him since I left and now that I'm almost home. He's at his place sound asleep." I complained. "He had told me he was going to be waiting for me at my place when I got back."

"But he had a call-out." She reasoned. "You have to cut him some slack."

"I know. But I get so little time alone with him." I whined.

"Where's the monster?"

"At her mother's until tomorrow afternoon. I just wanted some time for us. Brylee went to her dads for a few days, so we finally have a night that's just us."

"And he's asleep?"

"Always." I took a deep breath. "I've never seen someone who could sleep so much."

"He works hard." Shelly reminded me. "Don't be so hard on him. And don't say anything to make him feel bad."

"I won't." I promised. "So, what are you doing?"

"Brendon just went to bed. I was shutting things off downstairs and heading up when you called."

"I'm sorry. I didn't mean to keep you up. Do you want me to let you go?" I offered.

"Nah. Don't worry about it. I'm happy to keep you up."

"Thanks. I appreciate it. I just hit Avondale." I sighed heavily.

"You're almost there. Why don't you just go to Deuce's house?"

"Cause he's asleep and his mom's there. I don't want to bang on the door in the middle of the night trying to wake him up. My luck his mother will answer and considering I've never met her; this is not exactly the impression I'd like to make on her — the crazy new girlfriend beating on the door in the middle of the night for a booty call." I laughed.

"Good point." Shelly chuckled. "Perhaps waiting until tomorrow would be your best bet."

"As tired as I am, perhaps it is for the best. I'm going to be conscious for about five minutes after I return home anyway." Sad but true. I was in no condition to see anyone.

"You've had a long day. I can't believe you made that drive all by yourself. I'm not sure I could do it."

"After that hellish drive to Arizona three years ago, a four-teen-hour drive is nothing. Well, maybe not nothing, but doable anyway."

"Did you at least have fun?" She asked.

"I did. I love spending time with my kids. Sawyer is growing up so fast. I can't believe he is almost a year old. He's walking along the furniture and taking a few steps by himself. He's so determined to do things on his own. He's just like his father."

"You're so lucky. I can't wait to be a grandma. My son won't date anyone longer than a month. He enjoys being a bachelor." She said.

For a woman who was so enlightened, I didn't want to be the one to tell her Garrett was only occasionally dating to keep up appearances. He and his roommate, Xavier, were sharing more than just the rent.

"He'll find someone who makes him happy. Give him time." I swallowed hard.

"I hope so. He's 25. I'm tired of waiting." She giggled.

"Give him time. You want him to make the right choice and not settle down with the wrong person."

"How is Carson doing?"

"He just finished Airborne training, and he got into his master's program." I said proudly.

"That's wonderful. At least he's not being deployed anytime soon."

"He talked about that. I guess his unit is up for rotation so he might be sometime in the near future, but he's not sure when. I hate it."

"He's been deployed twice. Isn't that enough?"

"Some have been deployed five or more times. The military is short on soldiers, and this war is never going to end."

"I'm beginning to think you're right on that. I don't know how you do it. I couldn't let Garrett join the military." She told me.

"I'm proud of my son for serving his country; just like his father and most of the men in our family. He's a strong and honorable man. And yes, it scares the hell out of me, but he has my full support and love. What I hate is how much his deployments have changed him. He's not the same and probably never will be again. He's lost his smile. I just hope he finds it again." I explained.

"I couldn't let my son do it." She stated. "It's not worth it."

"Then where would our country be if all mother's felt that way? Freedom isn't free. It comes at a very high price. The military did Carson a world of good. He was my wild child. He wasn't ready for college when he finished high school. And look at him now; he's getting his master's. And he doesn't have the student loans that I do." I laughed.

"Garrett quit college after one semester. He's too intelligent, like me." It was a good thing she couldn't see me rolling my eyes. We held very different beliefs regarding formal education.

"I mean, I got my bachelor's in business and started my masters, but my professors were so rigid. They thought there was only one way to do things with their theories, concepts, and all that crap. To me, it was a waste of time and money, and I wanted to get on with building my business than studying hypotheticals." Shelly concluded.

"And yet you hired someone with an advanced degree when your business was in trouble." I reminded her.

"Fair enough, but you'll be paying student loans for the rest of your career." She chuckled.

"Career? More like the rest of my life. I'll die with student loan debt." I snickered, but it was a sad truth.

"Okay, enough of the heavy. I'm glad you got to see your family for the holiday. I know it's hard being away from them. I would be heartbroken if Garrett moved across the country."

"The Army didn't exactly ask me where I want my son stationed." I laughed. "You pretty much get told. It sucks, but we try to see each other as much as possible."

"I'm surprised you haven't moved to Nashville to be closer to them."

"Carson is an adult. And a soldier. He gets moved around every couple of years. I can't follow him. I have to let him have his own life."

"Well, I let Garrett have his own life, but I also like that I still get to see him every day."

"You work with your son. He still comes over for dinner several nights a week. He's 25 years old. Don't you think it's time to cut the umbilical cord?" It was not the first time I teased her about the unusually close bond she shared with her son.

"That's not fair. You have Brylee too. Garrett is all I have." She defended.

"Brylee works all the time. She's in school and is hardly ever home." I reminded her. "I'm happy that she has her own life. It's hard letting her go, but she's 22. She's spreading her wings and creating her own world. And I'm happy for her."

"Well, at least Deuce will be giving you another one to raise.

So, even when Brylee moves out, you'll still have a child at home."

"What?"

"Madelyn."

"Madelyn is Deuce's daughter. Not mine. We just started dating." I reminded her.

"You're awfully attached to him for someone you just started dating."

"Like you're not attached to Brendon?" I teased her.

"Perhaps a little." She admitted as I finally pulled in my place.

"I'm home." I announced turning the car off. "Thanks for getting me here."

"Isn't that what sisters are for?"

"Of course." I grabbed my bags out of the trunk. "I do appreciate it. I'm going to take a hot shower and collapse." I unlocked the front door.

Deuce was sitting on my couch with his stocking feet up on my coffee table. I was shocked.

"Oh, my God!" I dropped everything as Deuce stood up and jumped into his arms. "I can't believe you're here!" I kissed him through my tears.

"How could I not be? I've been waiting anxiously for you to come home." He kissed me again and brushed the tears off my cheeks. "I've missed you."

"I missed you too."

"I love you so much." I embraced him tightly. I never wanted to let him go.

"I love you." I whispered breathlessly in his ear. "Ah, crap. Shelly." I reached down and picked up my phone. "Hey, sorry about that. Deuce is here." I announced. "He surprised me."

"Good. I'm happy for you. Have fun tonight." She giggled.

"Thanks for everything, darling." I hung up the phone and tossed it on the couch.

"I'm so glad you're home." He took me by the hand and led me to my room.

"I need a shower. I feel gross." I complained. "Want to join me?" I smiled at him coyly.

"Definitely."

We undressed slowly. Both of us were exhausted and barely moving. My arms and legs felt like lead. I turned on the shower and grabbed us a couple clean towels from the linen closet.

The hot water rained down upon us like a warm blanket. I closed my eyes under the water and leaned back against Deuce's body. He felt solid and strong. He wrapped his arms around me and kissed my shoulder. I melted into him. He was a part of me.

We crawled into bed and snuggled up together. I rested my head upon his chest and traced my fingers lightly over his abdomen. I had missed the steady rhythm of his heartbeat and the feel of his warm skin against mine.

My hand traced down his little happy trail. Deuce's cock was standing at attention. I wrapped my fingers around it and squeezed it gently.

"Tease." He whispered.

"Always." I smiled up at him and climbed up on him.

I straddled him and kissed him deeply. I maneuvered myself and slowly lowered my body onto him. He slid into me with a hunger and eagerness that took my breath away. He held my hips and thrust his body deeply into me. It felt like forever since we'd been together

Deuce groaned loudly and tightened his grip on me.

"You didn't." I opened my eyes and stared down at him. "You did." I rolled my eyes in disbelief. "I can't believe you did."

"I'm sorry." He sighed heavily. "I didn't mean to, but it's been over a week, and you know it drives me crazy and makes me cum when you wiggle your ass like that."

I can't believe you." I rolled off him and flopped down on the pillow beside him.

"I'm sorry." He closed his eyes, looking as tired as I felt.

"You normally have such great stamina." I couldn't believe it.

"It's been over a week."

"I know, but still." I was at a loss for words.

"I know." He reached over and touched my arm lightly. "I'm so exhausted. I promise I'll make it up to you."

"You will, or you're going to tonight? I've been waiting a week as well." I pouted as I rolled over and propped myself up on my elbows facing him. "You're just going to leave me hanging?" I playfully traced my finger around his nipple.

"I'm tired." Deuce whined.

"Seriously?" I raised my eyebrows with a wicked smile. "You're going to do that to me?"

"Arya ..."

"No." I shook my head playing with him. "If you even think of falling asleep on me after it took you an entire minute and a half to get off, I swear I will wait until you fall asleep and I will get my tweezers out, and I will pull every single one of the hairs out of the crack of your ass all the way up to your scrotum." I told him with an evil grin while tugging a bit on the hairs on his chest.

"Damn, woman. You are evil! How sadistic can you be?" He reached over and started tickling me.

"It's your fault. You knew I had a psych degree." I laughed, trying to squirm away from him.

"But I never would have imagined you'd be so sick and twisted." He pinned me down, still tickling me.

"You love me." I proclaimed.

"Yes, but you seem hell bent on hurting me." He kissed roughly.

"No. Just collecting on what you owe me." I loved tormenting him. "And making you pay."

"So, if I give you an orgasm, you'll let me go to sleep?"

"Yep." I grinned. "Are you up for the challenge?"

"I've never had any problems with it before in the past." A devilish grin spread across his lips.

Deuce slid down my body, pausing to kiss my breasts, my abdomen. He teased me playfully in a seductive manner. He reached my pelvic bone and teased my clitoris with his tongue. His fingers traced over the inside of my thighs with a feather-like touch. He pushed two fingers inside me and pressed them against my G-spot.

I arched my hips towards him and moaned loudly. I dearly missed his touch and the way he teased me. My body ached for him. His tongue tormented me deliciously. I felt the pressure building within me, deep in my soul. My body fell into ecstasy.

I drifted into a deep and satisfying sleep with my body entangled around Deuce. Our bodies intertwined. Our hearts beating as one. I knew with every ounce of my soul, this was where I belonged. I had waited so long for this man. Not just the time I was gone on my trip, but my whole life. He was the one person in this world made just for me. He wasn't a perfect man, far from it, but he was the perfect man for me.

NINETEEN

WEDNESDAY EVENING, I PICKED Brylee up at the airport. She was flying in on the five o'clock from San Francisco, and I was supposed to pick her up outside the arrival's terminal. I had only been to the Phoenix airport a couple of times and never driven there alone. Traffic was horrific, and I couldn't find the American Airlines terminal.

I was almost frustrated to tears after circling around for the third time when I finally saw her standing outside with her suitcase. I pulled up quickly and popped the trunk.

"Hello, baby girl. How was your flight?" I wrapped my arms around her before I helped her put her bags in the car.

"Good." She walked around and got in the passenger side. "But it's good to be home."

"I know what you mean." I wove my way through the cars and back into the crazy loops around the airport in search of the right exit to take. "I hate this place." I mumbled.

"I figured Deuce would be with you."

"He got called out." I finally found our exit and quickly got over before I missed it. "How are your grandparents doing?"

"Fine. Grandma just remodeled the living room. It's gorgeous. You'd love it."

"She always had good taste. I love what she did in the family room a couple years ago." I smiled over at my daughter. "I missed you."

"I'm sure you were too busy enjoying Deuce and an empty house to even notice I wasn't around." Brylee smirked.

"That's not true."

"You weren't enjoying your time alone with Deuce?" She raised her eyebrows at me.

"Well, yes. But I did notice you weren't there. And I did miss you." I smirked.

"I missed you too." She reached over and took my hand. "It's good to be home."

~

Deuce called shortly after we arrived back home. The seven-mile journey from the airport took us forty-five minutes in rush hour traffic. It was aggravating enough to make the Pope curse.

"Hi, babe." I was happy to hear his voice.

"I'm going to kill you." He said cheerfully.

"What did I do now?" I set my purse down on the dining room table and watched Brylee fighting to get DaVinci on his lease.

"Guess who's here?"

"How would I know?" I was completely confused.

"Needles!"

"Oh, my God! Are you serious?" I busted out laughing.

"Yes."

"And it's your fault I can't get Miranda to get anything done."

"How is that my fault?"

"I told her what you said." He confessed.

"You weren't supposed to tell anyone." I giggled. "That's on you."

"I had to. It was the first thing I thought of when he arrived. Now she won't stop laughing." He explained. "My Lieutenant came over and asked what was so funny. Do you realize how hard it was to try to hold it together with her literally snorting behind me?"

"I'm sorry." I almost snorted myself.

"Good Lord, woman. You kill me." He chuckled. "Anyway, did you get Brylee?"

"Yes. We just got home."

"I'll be leaving here in about twenty minutes or so Do you want me to pick up something to eat?" Deuce offered.

"I can order some Chinese. Brylee already suggested it."

"Okay, that sounds good. I need a shower. It's hotter than Hades out here."

"All right. I'll wait until you're here to order it."

"Don't wait for me. It could take longer, and I don't want you both holding dinner on my account. I'll eat when I get there." He told me.

"Are you sure? We don't mind."

"Nah. Order it now. I'll be there as soon as I can."

"Okay. Please be careful."

"I will. I love you."

"I love you too."

I hung up the phone and called our favorite Chinese food from this little mom n' pop place around the corner. Knowing how unpredictable Deuce's schedule could be, I knew it could be more than an hour or so before he turned up. I was starting to become accustomed to this nontraditional lifestyle I suddenly found myself in.

Deuce finally showed up shortly before eight. He was exhausted and sweaty from standing outside in the triple digits for the last nine hours. DaVinci was going ballistic, per usual, when he arrived, so I asked Brylee to take him on a short walk.

"Are you going to jump into the shower with me?" Deuce asked, already removing his shirt as he walked into my room.

"If you want me too," I followed him and closed the door behind us.

Deuce stripped out of his dress clothes and leaned down for a quick kiss.

"Ugh. You stink." I playfully pushed him away.

"Come here, baby. Don't you want to kiss me?" He laughed and chased me around the bed.

"No." I scrambled to get away from him.

I managed to maneuver my way over to the bathroom and got the shower turned on. I jumped in quickly with Deuce right behind me.

"Here." I handed him the shampoo as I poured some body wash on the luffa.

I enjoyed tormenting him as I lathered him up. I scrubbed him down with the luffa and traced my other hand lightly over his body. He leaned back under the hot water and closed his eyes. I could feel how tense his muscles were, but the more I gently rubbed my fingers over them, his body began to relax.

"That feels so good." He exhaled softly.

"Good."

"You spoil me." A small tired smile spread across his shapely lips.

"Isn't it my job to take care of you." I whispered softly kissing him lightly on the cheek.

"You're good at it." He sighed with exhaustion. "I love you, Arya." He whispered.

"I love you too."

Deuce wrapped his arms around me and held me close as the

water rained down upon us. I closed my eyes and rested my head against his chest. I adored this man more than anything.

"You bitch!" The shower curtain was ripped back with such force half of it was torn off the rod.

My eyes flew open as I felt an abrupt pull of my hair and lost my footing. I screamed as I fell over the side of the tub. I felt a sharp sting to the side of my face, and my scalp felt as if it was on fire.

"I told you to stay away from him. He's mine!" The words barely registered as pain shot through my body, and my ears rang.

"What the fuck!" I heard Deuce shout. "Amber, stop!" A sudden jerk ripped my hair, and a final blow landed on the side of my back. I screamed out in pain.

I heard muffled yelling not far from me, but the blows had stopped. I reached up for a towel and tried to wrap it around myself. My ears were ringing. I looked past my vanity and realized Deuce was restraining Amber as the two of them yelled at each other.

"What the hell do you think you're doing?" He had her in a therapeutic hold.

"I told her to stay away from you. You belong to me. She didn't listen." Amber spat.

I struggled to my feet realizing quickly there was blood running down my face. I grabbed my robe off the back of the door and put the towel to my face. Brylee came running in with DaVinci barking louder than the constant barrage of profanity spewing from Amber.

"Put DaVinci in your room, Brylee." My daughter turned and stared at me but didn't move. "Brylee?" I raised my voice. "Put DaVinci in your room. Please!"

Brylee reached down and picked up her dog and hurried out of the room. I vaguely heard the sound of her door slam before she returned.

"Get my phone." I told her glaring at Amber.

"Who is she?"

Deuce was struggling to maintain his hold on Amber. She was kicking wildly and squirming about like a wild animal. His face was blood red. I'd never seen him so mad.

"His ex."

"Wife?" Brylee looked dumbfounded.

"Brylee! My phone!" I shouted at her.

She raced off into the family room and returned promptly with my phone. "Here," she thrusted it at me.

"Thank you." I wiped some blood off my face with the towel and dialed 911.

Seven minutes later, two of Phoenix's finest were on my doorstep. Deuce, still naked, but shielded by his hold on Amber, was more pissed off than embarrassed. I was simply pissed.

The officers were friends of Deuce. One of them had worked with him when he was still on patrol. They swiftly arrested Amber for breaking and entering and assault and battery. She was still screaming when they drug her out of my home.

Brylee admitted she'd left the front door unlocked when she went to take DaVinci for a walk — just as she'd done countless times before with no repercussions. This time, however, there had been. When Amber tried the knob on my front door, she had discovered it opened. She had planned on confronting Deuce about his dismissal of her and his non-responsiveness, but upon finding us in the shower and hearing the words we exchange, enraged her and she attacked me.

I refused to go to the emergency room, although every part of my body hurt. Amber had literally ripped handfuls of hair out of my scalp to the point that my scalp was bleeding. My left eye and cheek were heavily bruised, but my nose, now purple, had finally stopped bleeding. I had a huge fat lip, and there was a small amount of blood from my left ear. But even that wasn't nearly as concerning to me as was the boot-shaped bruise over my left kidney where Amber had managed to kick me when Deuce dragged her away.

"I'm so sorry." Deuce sat down on the side of my bed next to me. "I can't believe she did this." He put a frozen bag of peas on the side of my face. "I sent Brylee to Target to get a steak for your face. It'll still bruise, but it will get rid of the swelling."

"She's crazy." I muttered. "I hope they keep her locked up for a while."

"Even if she gets out on bail, I'll file a restraining order tomorrow morning to keep her away from you and Brylee." He assured me.

"And away from you, too." I told him.

"I can take care of myself." He half smiled.

"I know you can. I was thinking about Madelyn. I don't want to take the chance of her getting near her." I told him.

"All right. I'll file it for all of us. But I'll need you and Brylee to come down to sign the papers."

"Why does Brylee need to? She's my daughter."

"She's an adult." He reminded me.

"Okay." I was to mentally and physically drained to discuss it. "This is going to look great for my meetings tomorrow." My eyes welled up with tears. "How am I going to explain this?"

"Just say you were mugged." His sympathetic eyes implored.

"I can't believe this. Never in all my life ..." my voice trailed off.

"I can't tell you how sorry I am. I never would have imagined she'd do something like this. If I had any indication, I promise, I would have answered one of her phone calls."

"You couldn't have known." I tried to close my eyes, but it hurt. "I will say something, though."

"What's that?"

"Your prior taste in women leaves a lot to be desired." I tried to crack a smile but only winced from the pain.

"Thankfully, I finally found a great lady. The right one for me." Deuce leaned down and kissed me gently on my forehead.

~

Brylee stayed home with me the next day. I stayed in bed most of it and slept as much as my aching body would allow. My entire body was in pain from being ripped out of the shower to where each blow and kick had landed. I was covered in bruises and scrapes from my shins to my scalp; even my knees were black and blue from hitting the ceramic tile on the bathroom floor so hard. Brushing my hair brought me to tears.

I was battered, bruised, and pissed. The only time I managed to get up was when Deuce showed up mid-morning to take Brylee and me down to the precinct to sign the petition for a restraining order against Amber. I wasn't sure where she was being held, and I hadn't bothered to inquire if she'd been released yet. I honestly didn't care either way as long as she stayed away from us.

I spent an hour Friday morning with the CEO explaining the elaborate concoction Deuce had cooked up to explain my injuries. I felt horrible for lying, but I wasn't about to confess that the new man in my life had a psychotic ex-girlfriend that broke into my house and attacked me while I was in the shower with him.

It sounded absurd even to me. And at forty-five years young it was one of the last things I ever thought I'd have to contend with. I wasn't upset with Deuce but couldn't fathom how he had spent more than three years of his life with someone like her. He had said they'd had a tumultuous relationship that was more off than on.

From what I understood, Amber was temperamental at best. As far as he knew she wasn't suffering from bipolar or anything of that nature, she was simply just a bitch and enjoyed being one. Apparently, she was passing that trait on to her daughter as well who appeared to have an extreme dislike for Madelyn as well.

Of course, through my own experiences, I knew Madelyn had the tendency to make others want to lash out irrationally at her most of the time.

Renee knocked on my door not long after my humiliating meeting with the CEO. She poked her head in with a weary smile.

"I heard what happened. Are you okay?"

"Good morning, Renee. I'm all right; just sore.' I eased myself down into my chair with a grimace.

"I found something that I believe belongs to you." Her smile widened. "He was wondering the halls looking like a lost puppy."

"Excuse me," Renee stepped aside and let Deuce pass by her.

"Good morning, babe. I brought you some coffee. A skinny caramel macchiato over ice." He handed it to me and kissed me lightly on the cheek. "How are you feeling?"

"Sore, but fine." I grinned up into his brilliant blue eyes.

"You should have stayed home another day." I playfully rolled my eyes at him.

"Did you meet my right hand around here, Renee?" I gestured towards Renee lingering in the door.

"It's nice to finally meet you. I've heard a lot of good things about you." Renee approached Deuce and shook his hand.

"Likewise." Deuce leaned against the corner of my desk. "Tell me, does she push you as hard as she pushes herself?"

"Always." Renee laughed.

"Hey, just because you like to sit around and eat donuts all day does not mean the rest of us get to." I teased.

"I don't eat donuts," He stated with a cocky grin. "Or bagels for that matter."

"No. You just fill up on Dr. Pepper's and Swedish Fish." A truth I'd learned.

"Oh, screw you." Deuce playfully gave me the finger.

"I heard you had an interesting call-out on Wednesday." Renee remarked, walking over towards my desk with a smirk.

"You told her?"

"About you running into Needles?" I tried not to laugh and shrugged. "I had to. It was too funny not to share."

"It was embarrassing." He shook his head slightly with a grin. "I couldn't even look at the guy. All I wanted to do was walk up to him and say, 'hey man, I'm sorry' and walk away."

"The important thing is, you didn't." I tried to remain composed.

"You don't understand. I have to work with this man, and technically, he outranks me. And Miranda made it ten times worse. She couldn't stop laughing." He rolled his eyes in a humorous disgusted gesture. "She kept going; 'there's no bulge.' I had to literally smack her hand to keep her from pointing. Even my Lieutenant came over and questioned what we were laughing at and why we couldn't control ourselves." He pointed his finger at me. "And it's your fault."

"Then you should have told him the truth." I said as innocently as I could muster.

"Right. 'Sorry, Lieutenant. We're laughing because Wagner over there has a needle-size penis'. I'm sure that would have gone over well."

"You would think he has to know. I'm sure it's not the first time he's heard that." Renee stated.

"I don't think my Lieutenant and Wagner are that close." Deuce scoffed.

"No, moron. Wagner. He's got to know he's packing nothing

bigger than a baby carrot." I failed miserably at keeping a straight face.

"I told you, men don't look." He reiterated.

"I call bullshit." Renee pipped in. "Maybe men don't look at other men in the locker rooms or bathrooms or whatever, but I have never met a man who did not, at some point in his life, watch porn." I loved her cocky matter-of-fact attitude. "There is no way he does not know that he's packing a teaser, not a pleaser."

"I agree. He would have to know." I doubled over laughing at her words.

"I'm sure at some point in his life, some woman has complained." Renee looked from me to Deuce in a questioning manner. "I mean, how could you not. You wouldn't be able to feel it." She raised her pinky for emphasis. "That's just sad."

"Women are mean." Deuce couldn't keep it together. His face was bright red as he lost control.

"You say mean. I say honest." Renee told him.

"I agree." I nodded at her. "Why shouldn't we be able to say something?"

"It's not like he can control the size of his cock." Deuce wiped the tears of laughter off his cheeks.

"Well, he can do what men expect women with small breasts to do." Renee told him. "He can get implants."

"Ouch." Deuce's hand automatically dropped to cover his crotch. "That's harsh."

"Why? Women get implants all the time to please men. Why shouldn't men with Chapstick-sized penis' do the same?" I asked.

"Because it's completely different. That's not an area you want someone with a scalpel." He declared.

"And you think it's a jolly ol' time getting your breasts sliced up to please a man? But women do it every day." Renee grinned at Deuce.

"That just proves women are stupid." Deuce shrugged with a chuckled. "Men aren't that dumb. If a woman doesn't like the size of our cock, we'll just find one that does."

"Damn. Talk about cold." I was stunned, but only by the truthfulness of his words. "I guess that explains why he's been married twice. He's still trying to find one who won't complain."

"You can't laugh. You've been divorced too." He glanced over at me.

"So, has she." I nodded at Renee.

"Hey, I'm still looking for the perfect man." Renee explained.

"And is size a deal-breaker for you?" Deuce asked with a cocky grin.

"I can deal with small, but Chapstick-size. No. That would be a deal-breaker for me. I don't want to be under a man who thinks he's blowing my mind when in fact, I can only tell he's making an effort because he's on top of me, and not because I can feel anything." She answered, honestly.

"What if he's the greatest guy you've ever met and is everything you've ever wanted in every other way?" Deuce was having fun toying with her.

"Then I'd be a frequent shopper at Fascinations." She shrugged. "But no. I'm sorry. Maybe I'm too shallow of a person, but I couldn't do it. Sex is everything in a relationship, but it's too important to not exist at all."

"Don't look at me, I completely agree with her." I concurred when Deuce shifted his gaze to see my reaction.

"Women are brutal." He stated.

"Are you going to tell me that sex isn't that important to you?" I gave me a devious smile.

"I didn't say that at all." He smirked back at me. "And as much as I'm enjoying this conversation, I've got to get back to work." Deuce picked up his coffee. "I'll be home around one thirty."

I walked around my desk and wrapped my arms around him. "Thank you for the coffee." I kissed him sweetly.

"I was a bit curious about where you disappear to every day." He teased.

"Yeah, well, don't be surprised if I return the favor someday." I told him.

"Good luck getting in the building." He let me go and turned towards Renee. "It was nice meeting you. Have a great weekend."

"Thanks. You too." She waved as I walked him to my office door.

"Be careful. I'll see you in a bit."

"I will. I love you."

"I love you, too." I kissed him goodbye once more before I closed my door behind him.

"He's adorable." Renee said before I reached my desk.

~

I left the office at one hoping to beat the early rush of traffic on a Friday afternoon. Typically, the traffic in Phoenix wasn't bad during the summer months as all the insufferable snowbirds had flown the coup by the end of May. I was coasting along with the air conditioning and the radio blasting through my car. It was a beautiful summer day with clear blue skies touching down on the mountain tops without a cloud in sight.

I was singing along poorly with Elton John when I was abruptly interrupted by an incoming call. Without looking, I begrudgingly hit the answer button on my steering wheel.

"Hello, baby girl. How are you?" Ryan's sultry voice filled my car.

"I'm good. How are you?" I didn't want to tell him about the incident with Amber as he would undoubtedly use it as ammunition against Deuce.

"Ticked off." But I could hear the playfulness in his voice.

"And why is that?"

"Because you owe me an apology." The infamous text message Deuce had sent him suddenly entered my mind.

"Yes, I do. And I apologize. I saw what Deuce sent you and while I'm not making any excuses for what he did, he did just get back from a double homicide call-out and wasn't in a very good mood. Not to mention his ex-girlfriend has been blowing up his phone." I explained.

"Regardless, it was rude."

"Yes, it was. I'm sorry."

"Is he that jealous?" Ryan asked.

"He claims he's not a jealous man, but that text certainly disagreed."

"And why is his ex calling? When did they split up?"

"Last December. She's a bit neurotic." What a mild understatement.

"You could just let him go to be with her, and then we can be together." I could picture the cocky smile on his face.

"You're terrible."

"You wouldn't change me." He laughed.

"No, I wouldn't."

"Are you at the office or at home?"

"I'm on my way home from the office." I told him.

"Any big plans for the weekend?"

"Nope. He's picking up his daughter tomorrow so ..." I let my voice trail off in exasperation.

"So, after working hard all week long, you get rewarded with taking care of his kid. Sounds fun, Arya. Is this what you really want?"

"Please don't, Ryan. I'm struggling enough with the fact that we can't go anywhere or do anything." I begged him.

"I simply don't see the intrigue here. He's never going to be able to give you what you want. He's not in the same league as you." Ryan argued.

"What league?" I was quickly getting annoyed.

"Every league, Arya. Why can't you see that?"

"What am I supposed to be seeing?"

"You've got a Ph.D. Didn't you say he only had a semester of college before he dropped out?"

"Yeah. So?"

"So? You're miles ahead of him just in education?"

"Your logic sucks considering you keep telling me how I belong with you and you didn't even do a single semester." I reminded.

"But we have fun together." He argued. "When's the last time you really had fun with him? Does he take you to concerts? Festivals? Trips to the mountains or the ocean like I did? No. He's too busy playing mommy and daddy to a spoiled brat because his ex-wife is a narcissist psychopath."

"Ryan ..." I started but couldn't find a reasonable argument.

"You know I'm right."

"I'm not saying you're wrong." Suddenly the bruises on the side of my face started throbbing, and my head went to instant migraine.

"Then have dinner with me tonight. We can talk. Or better yet; let's go to San Diego for the weekend. You know we'd have a blast."

"I can't." Even if I wanted to, there was no way I would ever let Ryan see me like this. But that didn't make a difference either because my heart, body, and soul belonged to Deuce and he was the only man I wanted despite all the bullshit.

"Yes, you can. You're not married, Arya.

"I don't need a ring, Ryan. I love him. I won't cheat on him or hurt him like that." I heard Ryan sigh heavily.

"I won't give up."

"Have a good weekend, Ryan.

"Call me if you change your mind."

"Goodbye, Ryan." I disconnected the call and pulled up to my place.

All I wanted to do was take a refreshing shower and crawl into bed. My head was pounding. Ryan's words hurt more than I was willing to admit. I knew there was a great deal of truth in them. I knew that Deuce would never be able to run freely and that the responsibilities he had were more than most. But I also knew that I wanted to be the one beside him to hopefully ease some of that burden off his broad shoulders.

I knew it wasn't going to be easy. Anything worth having never was. I believed in my heart that Deuce was worth it, Madelyn too. She simply needed some guidance, love, compassion, boundaries, and discipline. But we would get there, in time. Nothing was going to change overnight. I knew that much. However, in my heart, I knew Deuce was worth it. He was everything.

TWENTY

DEUCE AND I STAYED IN for the evening. I wasn't feeling well when he arrived home shortly after me. I didn't tell him about my conversation with Ryan. I knew it would only upset him. Plus, the way my head was pounding I wasn't in the mood to have a debate with him over the man I used to sleep with.

Instead, we curled up in bed and turned on *Outlander* on Starz. It was my favorite book series, and I was in love with Sam Heughan from the series. Deuce had never seen the series, so I was determined to introduce him to it.

"I wish we could stay like this all weekend." I snuggled up next to him with my head on his chest.

"We can — at least until tomorrow morning. I have to pick up Madelyn at nine." Deuce stroked my hair softly.

"Okay." I sighed heavily.

"What's wrong?" I wasn't sure if I should say anything or not.

"Do you realize that we've never had a weekend together since Madelyn got back from Wisconsin? I just think it would be nice if we could actually have some time alone." I tried to put it as gently as I could.

"Cathy is supposed to keep her one weekend a month, but she doesn't exactly honor it. And I don't push her to either." He confessed.

"It's okay." I tried to hide my disappointment.

"No, it's not." He gave me a gentle squeeze. "What would you say if I talk to Cathy and have her keep Madelyn next weekend and we can head up to the Sonoran Desert for the weekend."

"Are you serious?" I leaned up and looked at him.

"We can leave Friday evening and come back Sunday afternoon. What do you think?"

"I think I'd love too." I reached up and kissed him.

"Good. Then it's settled." He smiled. "I can't believe you've lived down here for three years and haven't gone."

"I haven't had a chance. I've been working." I smirked.

"It's amazing. You'll love it."

"I can't wait." I snuggled into him.

My head was starting to feel a bit better, and my heart was feeling much better. I couldn't wait to spend some time alone with Deuce. It felt like an eternity since we'd spent that first week together. I cared a great deal for Madelyn, but I wanted to be selfish once in a while.

~

Sunday morning, I woke up early to play golf with Shelly. I was feeling better, although I wasn't looking much better. I spent the first four holes explaining to her the joys of Deuce's psychotic ex-girlfriend. Initially, she acted concerned and listened attentively. Then she flipped a switch and turned into someone I didn't even recognize.

"You know, Brendon cautioned me about the Phoenix PD." She stated matter-of-factly. "This just proves he was right."

"What's that supposed to mean?"

"Look what happened to you." She pointed towards my face.

"How exactly is that Deuce's fault?"

"He brought crazy into your life."

"Can't you say the same thing about Brendon?" I tried to laugh it off. "And he's bringing a lot more baggage and crazies into your life."

"Well, as long as you're with him, there's no way we can ever do couples golf or even double date for dinner and a movie. Brendon hates the police, and I can't say I'm too fond of them." She tossed her blond hair over her shoulder.

"Aren't you the one who encouraged me to give him a chance?" I couldn't believe she was acting this way.

"That was before you got your ass beat for it." She scoffed.

"He didn't do it. He restrained the bitch." I felt defensive, and I'm not sure why.

"Look, if you want to keep dating the pig; that's entirely up to you, but from now on I don't want to hear about it." I couldn't believe what I was hearing.

"What is going on with you?"

"I'm sorry, Arya, but Brendon and I live together. We are in a serious relationship. Deuce is barely a boyfriend you've been dating for less than two months." She put her hand on my arm with fake sincerity. "You're one of my closest friends, and I value our friendship. I hope you don't throw it all away on a crush."

"Wow. Seriously? You are unbelievable." I felt like she'd slapped me across the face.

We had just reached the seventh hole, and Shelly climbed out of the cart with her driver. "I hope you make the right decision." She smirked.

I bit my tongue hard enough to draw blood as we teed off. I was silently fuming as we climbed back into the cart and set off in search of our balls. Thankfully, we found hers first, and she got out and selected her club.

I sat there in the driver's seat, watching her smug face as she flipped her hair over her shoulder and took a couple practice swings. My eyes narrowed at Shelly, and my foot hit the gas pedal. I knew she thought I was going off in search of my ball, but instead I hopped back onto the golf cart pathway and headed back to the clubhouse. Unfortunately, her golf bag was still strapped into the back.

I pulled up to the cart return and retrieved my bag. I left Shelly's and headed to my car. I'd reached my limit and could have cared less how upset Shelly was being left on the course. I stuck my bag in the trunk and slammed it shut. I felt wonderful.

I told Deuce about my conversation with Shelly. He felt bad that he was the cause of our argument. I assured him repeatedly that he wasn't. If anyone was to blame for our disagreement, it was Brendon. I trust my gut, and my gut was screaming at me that he was nothing but trouble.

The multiple lies and half-truths he filled her head with somehow did not add up to me. Her low self-esteem and gullibility made her easy prey for con-artists, predators, and criminals. She was well experienced in each of those categories, and it did not appear she was interested in changing her behavior.

~

WEDNESDAY EVENING, I had a feeling something was wrong. Deuce didn't like to spend time at the mall, let alone shopping, but voluntarily offered to go to the mall with me to shop for a gift for my grandson's first birthday. I had an uneasy feeling in my stomach as I stood beside him while he browsed through the bookshelves. He had been quiet most of the evening. He purchased a couple military magazines and took my hand.

"I got a call from Cathy this afternoon. She made plans for this weekend. So, I have to pick up Madelyn on Friday."

"Shocker." I said low enough for him not to hear me. I took a deep breath and bit my bottom lip. "Okay."

"I'm sorry. I know we were supposed to go to Secona, and now we can't. But I promise I'll make it up to you."

"What came up?" I was so sick of this woman I could scream. She was the most pathetic excuse for a mother.

"A party." He said quietly.

"A party? Are you serious?" I took a deep breath.

"I know." Deuce half shrugged in an almost defeated manner. "But what am I supposed to do? She's my daughter, and if I have the chance to get her away from that crazy bitch, I'm going to take it."

"I understand." And I did, but it still irritated me simply because I was looking forward to our trip.

"I promise, I'll make it up to you."

"I know." I squeezed his hand.

I knew he would — eventually.

Whether he'd ever get the opportunity remained to be seen.

"Not to sound like a bitch, but did you happen to mention to Madelyn that we were going away this weekend?" I asked.

"Yes." It took a couple seconds for the light bulb to go on. "Oh. I see what you're saying." Deuce sighed heavily. "Madelyn didn't do it on purpose."

"I know, but Cathy is." I pointed out.

"Yes. She is." He squeezed my hand. "I'm sorry."

"I don't blame you."

"Please don't be upset with Madelyn either." He looked at me imploringly.

"I'm not. I'm just tired of Cathy's crap."

"I know. Me too. And from what I understand, Jason isn't going with her either." He shrugged. "I'm not surprised. Madelyn said they fight all the time and he's hardly ever home."

"Who's Jason?"

"Cathy's third husband."

"She went from Grayson to Jason?" I giggled.

"Yeah, I know. It's ridiculous. I told you, she's like that line from *Suicide Squad*; 'fifteen pounds of crazy in a ten-pound bag.'" He rolled his eyes. "Tony and Ernesto believe he's my doppelganger."

"Huh? Is he a cop too?"

"No. I think he's a pharmacist or something. But they both claim he's my long-lost twin." His mouth twitched. "You know, they say everyone has a twin out there, and they give me grief that he's mine."

"Seriously?" He nodded. "That's creepy."

We walked by the Disney Store and pulled my phone out of my purse. "What's Cathy's new last name?" I pulled up my Facebook app.

"Why?"

"I'm curious."

"Finkle"

"Ugh." I giggled and typed it in.

Cathy's profile immediately popped up. I clicked on photos and started browsing. I had never seen her before or even a photo of her, but Madelyn indeed looked a great deal like her mother. But she had Deuce's stunning blue eyes.

Cathy looked like she was probably about my height and a bit heavier than me. She had mousey brown hair and a big nose. She wasn't what I would have considered to be attractive, but she wasn't homely either. Her pictures were almost all selfies she'd taken. With her mental issues, that didn't surprise me at all. She had only a couple pictures of Madelyn and another older boy who I assumed to be her son from her first husband, Caleb.

Finally, I found a picture of her and Jason. I was so shocked I almost dropped my phone. If it weren't for the blue eyes, I would have sworn it was a photo of Cathy and Deuce. Jason had blue eyes, but they were nowhere nearly as brilliant as Deuce's. The resemblance between the two was downright creepy.

"Tony and Ernesto weren't kidding." I held my phone over for him to see.

"I know. I told you she was sick and twisted in the head."

"That's an understatement." I muttered, staring at the photo. "This doesn't bother you?"

"What can I do about it?" He shrugged nonchalantly.

"I don't know, but that's just wrong. It's creepy."

"I guess."

"I'm guessing she didn't want the divorce?" I looked over at him.

"No. I did. I couldn't take it anymore. I tried for Madelyn and Caleb's sake, but I just couldn't do it anymore. Her antics were too much."

"Wow. And here I thought Amber was my biggest problem." I muttered under my breath.

We finished off our evening without buying anything but instead went to the Cheesecake Factory for dinner. We tried to make the best of the evening. However, neither of us could dismiss the melancholy cloud Cathy had cast over us.

I could almost feel the bitch sitting in her westside home, smiling and satisfied with herself.

~

Deuce dropped by the next afternoon unexpectedly. He was giddy and acting like a child on Christmas morning.

"What do you think of Vegas?" He kissed me when I opened the door.

"It's fun." I looked at him suspiciously.

"What about Vegas next weekend?"

"What about Madelyn?"

"My mom agreed to watch her." He grinned deviously pulling me to him.

"Are you serious?" I wrapped my arms around his neck.

"Absolutely. I already booked up a suite for us at New York New York." He kissed me firmly. "We'll take a long weekend; leave Thursday morning and come back Sunday." He kissed me again. "How does that sound?"

"Fabulous! I'm in."

We stumbled together groping and pulling at each other's clothes back into my bedroom. We tumbled onto my bed, with Deuce on top of me. I pulled his shirt over his head and tossed it aside. I ran my fingers over his bare chest, teasing his nipples.

Deuce leaned down over me and kissed the tip of my nose. "I could get used to this." He whispered.

"Me too." I stared into his crystal blue eyes.

Deuce moved his hand beneath my shirt and traced his fingers lightly over my stomach. I held my breath in anticipation. I knew how much he loved toying with me. Almost as much as I loved teasing him.

His hand moved slowly up to my breasts. He massaged one gently for a moment before lifting my bra up over it. He brought his lips to mine and kissed me hungrily. I could fee his hard, thick, cock throbbing against the outside of my thigh. I wanted him.

He rose a bit and pulled my shirt up over my head, tossing it aside carelessly. He swiftly removed my bra and nudged me backward on the bed. He playfully slid off the bed with a devilish grin across his shapely lips.

He stood before me, unfastened my shorts, and pulled them off. As I lay in nothing but my black lace panties looking at his majestic form before me.

Deuce slowly ran his hands lightly up my legs with is fingertips. It felt like little bolts of lightning coursing through me. My body ached for him. I reached out for his hand, but he smiled and shook his head.

"You're so mean." I whined.

"You love it." He grinned mischievously.

"Yes. I do."

His hands gravitated towards my hips. His fingers slipped beneath the sides of my panties. He took his sweet time pulling them leisurely down my legs and dropping them on the floor. His fingertips traced back up the inside of my legs, pushing them slightly apart.

I sighed deeply as he brushed teasingly over my lips and slipped his hands beneath me, firmly gripping my buttocks. In one swift motion, he pulled me to the edge of my bed.

Deuce's tongue lingered over the inside of my thighs, making me squirm. His fingers gently parted my lips, exposing my clitoris. He lapped at it teasingly and then took it into his mouth, sucking on it, sending waves of fire throughout my body.

I pressed up against him with desire. He pushed two fingers deep inside me, pressing against my G-spot. I could feel the orgasm building inside me; ready to explode. I arched my hips slowly as he moved his fingers in and out of me with one hand and caressing my ass with his other hand; holding me in place. He inserted a finger into my ass, driving me closer to the brink of insanity.

I inhaled deeply and let out a long moan. I reached for Deuce, but he refused to budge. My breathing quickened with his fingers moving in and out of me, his mouth and tongue devouring my clitoris. I was in heaven. The man knew exactly how to play my body like an instrument. I was completely his to do with as he pleased.

An eruption of pleasure swept over me that I was no longer able to contain. I screamed out in ecstasy as the orgasm rippled through my body. Deuce held on firmly to combat my thrashing about in my vague attempt to escape him. He continued until he knew I was mentally and physically spent.

Deuce stood up and shoved his rock-hard thick cock deep inside me. I screamed in delight as another wave coursed through my body. He firmly grabbed my hips with my legs against his upright chest, my feet resting on his shoulders, and thrust deeper and deeper inside me until his muscles tightened and he groaned loudly reaching his own orgasm.

My legs fell to the side as Deuce collapsed upon me. his weight crushed me briefly before he rolled off to my side.

"God, I love that you're multi-orgasmic." He smiled wickedly, still breathing heavily.

"I love that you know exactly how to please me." I ran my hands up and down his smooth skin, damp with perspiration.

"I can't imagine ever spending my life with anyone else. You are my everything." Deuce took my hand in his. "I love you more than words could ever express." He leaned down and kissed my fingers.

"I love you too, Grayson. And I do want to spend my life with you, and I will. I simply want to make this transition as easy as I can for all of us." I explained.

"I understand," he whispered. "Just promise me something."

"Anything."

"That we will start looking for a house and start planning our future together." His eyes pleaded with me lovingly.

"I'd love that." I leaned over to him, drawing him in close and kissed his shapely lips.

TWENTY-ONE

FRIDAY AFTERNOON, I WAS packing up my paperwork
for the weekend of things I needed to work on. The employees in
the accounting department were so averse to change that they
were making my job miserable. I was almost to the point of
replacing the entire department if their attitude didn't change.

Renee knocked on my door and leaned her head in.

"Arya? Do you have a minute?" She asked.

"Sure. Come on in." Renee took a seat in one of the chairs
across my desk.

"I wanted to drop off the marketing analysis that you request-
ed." She handed me a folder.

"Thanks. I'll take a look at these this weekend." I glanced at
the first couple of pages and then stuck it in my briefcase. "Also,
just so you know. I'm not going to be here next Thursday or
Friday. Deuce and I are going to Vegas for a long weekend."

"Sounds fun. And romantic." A sly smile crossed her lips,
and she raised her eyebrows at me.

"I hope so." I sat back down in my chair. "We could really use
some alone time without our daughters constantly underfoot."

"I understand that." She agreed.

"If you need me at all, you'll be able to reach me on my cell." I assured her.

"Yeah, but will you be sober enough?" She laughed.

"That, I can't promise you." I snickered.

"Good. Unless the place is on fire, I won't contact you." She promised. "You deserve a break and some time alone with him. He's one of the good ones." She smiled.

"Thanks. I think so too." I agreed.

"Are you two getting serious?"

"There are a few obstacles, but I believe so." I sighed. "I'm crazy about him."

"It shows. I've never seen you so happy."

"My son wants to meet him." I told her.

"And that's a bad thing?" Renee asked.

"My son is protective. He's older." I tapped the desk. "My son is 25, and Deuce's daughter is only 9. Not to mention, Brylee is 23. I've lived an entire lifetime of parenting experience in comparison to Deuce."

"That's true. But is that an asset or a curse?"

"Right now, it's a curse." I snorted.

"Why?"

"Because anytime I try to give him advice, I feel like he takes it like a personal attack." I answered, honestly.

"Are his parenting skills that bad?"

"You've dealt with a step-daughter, how did you handle it." I inquired.

"Not well at first, I admit." Renee shrugged. "My step-daughter was a source of constant battles between her father and me. She was an absolute terror at 13. Her favorite thing was to pit her father and me against each other. She was a perfect little puppet-master playing some sick little game."

"You're not making me feel any better about this whole step-parenting gig." I half giggled in a terrified way.

"Who knows, maybe you'll get lucky, and Madelyn is young enough that you two can develop a strong relationship. Hopefully, she isn't Satan like mine was."

"I don't believe Madelyn is Satan, but I do think she's a brat in need of serious discipline, structure, and consistency. I feel bad for her. She's got a rotten mom." I exhaled loudly. "I mean, this woman has done all kinds of emotional damage to this kid. Madelyn has been seeing a shrink for years. Deuce is trying to combat the damage." I explained.

"At least that's a good start."

"It is." I tapped my fingers again. "He tries, but it's like he's overcompensating and not in a good way. He lets this kid get away with murder with zero accountability for her behavior."

"You should talk to him about it."

"I've tried. He immediately jumps to the defensive whenever I bring it up. He sees it as a personal attack." I explained.

"He probably does when you consider he's been a single parent most of her life." She reminded me.

"Take it down a notch with the parenting advice. And pick and choose your battles." She smiled, wearily at me.

"I know you're right. But it's much harder than I imagined." I confessed. "Especially when I've seen first-hand what the consequences will be."

"Then allow him to pay the price for it." She stated. "He'll learn, just as you did."

"I know. Unfortunately, I have to sit on the sidelines and pay the price alongside him."

"Ah, the joys of dating a single dad." She tried to lighten the mood. "At least he's sexy as hell."

"True."

"Well, I've got to pick up my ungrateful's from daycare. You have a great weekend."

"Thanks, Renee. You too." She smiled and closed my door on her way out.

~

Deuce was waiting for me when I arrived home. He had already changed his clothes and was lounging on my bed reading a book. He looked comfortable and entirely at ease. I found myself wishing it could always be this way. I was already accustomed to sleeping beside him every night; I slept better with him beside me.

He smiled when I entered the room. I petted DaVinci for a moment and then sat down on the edge of the bed.

"How was your day?" I reached out and put my hand on his leg.

"It's Friday."

"Thank goodness. It's been a long week." I fell over sideways to land on the pillows beside him. "You hungry?"

"A little. You?"

"Yes. I skipped lunch." I confessed. "I've got a pile of paperwork to go through this weekend. I was trying to get a jump start on it."

"I'm looking forward to Thursday." Deuce said in a tired voice.

"Me too." I snuggled up into the nook under his arm. "Aren't you on-call on Sunday?" I was starting to adjust to his hectic schedule as well.

"Yep." He closed his book and set it on the nightstand. "Right now, I just want to lay here with you."

"I love that idea." I closed my eyes and listened to the steady rhythm of his heartbeat.

We went out for Mexican for dinner with Brylee. She was all excited about some new guy she'd met at a coffee shop near campus. She was dying to tell me all about him and eagerly accepted Deuce's invitation to join us.

Brylee babbled on throughout the entire meal about this guy named Damon. She told us about his wavy dark hair and big brown eyes, his smile, and biceps. It was cute hearing about her new crush. She hadn't had one in a long time. I was happy for her. They were planning on going to dinner together the following night.

Deuce and I jumped into the shower together once we returned home. He was in an unusually good mood for someone who was so exhausted earlier.

"So, is that what I get to look forward too?" He asked.

"The ramblings description of a cute guy at the coffee house?" I laughed and splashed some water in his face.

"Yeah," He laughed.

"Pretty much." I picked up the shampoo giving Deuce a playful nudge.

"Oh joy. I can't wait." He mocked and rolled his eyes.

After we toweled off, I put on a pair of my pink silk pajamas and followed Deuce out onto the balcony. The stars were shining brightly over the mountains to the west. The air was humid and dense. I walked up behind him and wrapped my arms around him.

"I love this." I whispered.

"Me too." He turned around and faced me. "Are you ready to go to bed?"

"Sure," I followed him back into my room.

"I'm going to grab a couple water bottles." He kissed me quickly, closing the door behind us. "Be right back."

I climbed under the covers and turned on the TV. My mind was exhausted, but my body was wide awake. Deuce returned and placed a water bottle on my nightstand and then one on his own.

"Thank you."

He walked over and turned off the lamp on my desk. My eyes followed him around the room. He had a mischievous look on his face, and I couldn't help but wonder what he was up too.

Deuce lifted the covers, his eyes sparkling in the soft glow. "And another thing, Ms. Lucas," I giggled at his serious tone. "I've followed your rules and played along with your game. But I've decided it's time you do as I say."

He leaned down and grabbed hold of my hips, pulling me over to where he stood beside the bed. His actions caught me off guard, catching my breath in my chest.

"You think so?" I smiled sounding cockier than I felt.

"I know so." He stated firmly.

Deuce roughly pulled my dusty pink silk pajama pants off and climbed up on the bed, straddling over me.

"You're in my world now and no longer the alpha — you belong to me." A devilish grin that slipped across his shapely lips intrigued me.

He held my bottoms over my chest and took hold of one of my wrists. "Let's see what you think of being helpless." His blue eyes twinkled.

"You are not going to ..." But the words caught in my throat as he quickly tied one leg of my pants around one wrist. Before I could say anything, he pinned my other wrist and swiftly tied the other.

I felt a tightening in my stomach that had nothing to do with the minimal weight of Deuce straddling me. I swallowed hard at the lump in my throat. I felt a cross between exhilaration and anxiety slashed with fear. I'd never been tied up before in my life. I'd never had anyone take total control over me in my life. I'd never been helpless.

Deuce slid down my body and pushed my legs wide apart. I reached up to touch his chest, as awkward as it was with my hands bound.

"Did I say you could touch me?" He swiftly smacked the side of my thigh, catching me completely off guard.

"Ouch!" I was shocked.

Deuce pulled my hands back over my head and tied the second pant leg of my pajama bottoms around the bedpost. He maneuvered his way back between my legs and leaned down, kissing my breasts rougher than he usually did and nibbled on my nipples. I squirmed beneath him. He lifted his eyes with a wicked twinkle I'd never seen before.

His lips and tongue glazed over my stomach as he moved his way down my body. He traced his fingers lightly over the inside of my thighs. The stubble on his face brushed roughly over my smooth skin. I inhaled deeply and closed my eyes savoring every moment of it.

I felt his tongue brush softly over my lips; his hot breath on my skin warming the core of my being. I arched my hips up towards him, and my blissful state was met with a sharp smack on the outside of my thigh.

"Be still," he whispered in a rough voice.

My muscles tensed for a second and then relaxed beneath him. My mind was whirling. He'd never acted this way before. I'd never seen this side of him. I'd always controlled things in this area of our life. I hated to admit I was captivated.

Deuce pushed my legs up and spread them wider apart. His tongue parted my lips and teased my clitoris. I fought the urge to move my hips and bit down hard on my bottom lip. I wanted to feel him deep inside me. I craved him desperately.

I felt his fingers part my lips as he brought his mouth to my clitoris and began suckling on it. Deuce abruptly pushed two fingers deep inside me. I gasped audibly.

I wanted to rock my hips with the rhythm of his fingers, but I didn't dare. I bit down harder on my lip and could taste the metallic taste of blood in my mouth.

"Damn, Deuce." I squirmed helplessly.

This new enticement awakened a helpless desire in me I had never experienced before. My movement caught his attention, and I was promptly rewarded with a smack to the outside of my thigh.

"Ouch!"

"I didn't say you could move." His eyes sparkled with delight in his newfound power.

"I can't help it." I pleaded.

"Arya, trust me." There was a rough sexiness to his tone.

"I do."

Deuce rolled me over on to my stomach. He ran his hands lightly up the back of my legs, landing them on my buttocks. He smacked each side sharply causing me to jump. Then he caressed them with his fingers and the palms of his hand, firmly yet gently.

I wanted desperately to squirm towards him, to arch my hips. But I bit my lower lip again and willed myself not to move. His hands traced along the insides of my thighs, pushing them slightly apart. I felt his fingers brush softly over my lips. I closed my eyes and felt the tension melt out of every muscle in my body as I fully submitted to him.

Deuce's fingers brushed lightly over my clit, rubbing it between two fingers. He teased me relentlessly before inserting them into me. I could feel the moisture from my desire for him welling up between my legs. He tormented my G-spot gloriously.

He readjusted himself between my legs, pushing them further apart. His hands slid beneath me, lifting me up on my knees with my shoulders and head still resting comfortably on the pillows, hands tied above my head.

Deuce knelt between my legs and spread my buttocks apart.

He headed down and kissed my lips. His tongue danced over my clitoris and delved into me. I loved the way he teased me.

I moaned loudly into the pillow, trying not to rock my hips. But then his fingers probed deeply into me again, and I closed my eyes, letting the world around me disappear in the pure animal-istic pleasure soaring through my body.

Deuce straightened back up and kneaded my buttocks with his hands once more before he leaned down again, leave a quick little kiss on each cheek.

Then I felt the head of his cock rubbing over my lips, extending my torment. His cock parted my lips as he teased me with just the head. With a quick and unexpected thrust, Deuce pushed himself fully deep inside me taking my breath away. I screamed out in pure delight.

Our rhythm quickly fell into place, and our bodies moved as one. I loved the way he filled me completely. He was the perfect size. No matter what position we were in, his cock managed to always find my G-spot. My body quivered in spasms. I could not get enough of him.

Deuce thrust repeatedly into me. His hands gripped tightly on my hips. He moaned behind me and smacked one of my buttocks sharply catching me off guard and snapping me abruptly out of my own euphoria.

He flipped me around like a rag doll. I was utterly helpless under his control. He placed my legs up on his shoulders, leaned down and crushed his mouth over mine. His tongue hungrily searched mine, dancing harmonically with mine.

Deuce adjusted his hips, forcing his cock back into me. My breath quickened as our bodies moved as one. His lips tenderly stroked mine. He slowed his movement slightly, savoring the sensation pulsating through him.

Then I felt his muscles tighten and become tense over me. His body jolted in quick spasms as I felt him cum deep inside me;

his cock throbbing uncontrollably. He held himself frozen for a moment before collapsing upon me.

"My legs." I barely squeaked.

"Oh. Sorry." Deuce lifted himself slightly allowing me to remove my legs from his shoulders.

"I love you." I wrapped my legs around his waist, holding him still inside me.

"I love you too." He whispered in a hoarse voice. He reached up and untied my wrists.

"Thanks." I smiled into his eyes and kissed him softly. "I don't ever want to lose you." I confessed.

"You never will."

TWENTY-TWO

SATURDAY AFTERNOON, DEUCE and I headed to the mall to look for some new sandals for me. I was looking for something casual and comfortable for our trip to Las Vegas. But I also wanted something cute and stylish. Something Deuce loved giving me grief about.

After the fifth store, he was getting a bit frustrated with me.

"How many more stores do we have to track through? Just pick something." He complained, lifting up a hideous white sandal that looked like something my grandmother wouldn't be caught dead in. "These look comfortable."

"You've got to be kidding me." I scoffed.

"You're telling me that style is more important than comfort?"

"Absolutely."

"That's ridiculous." He rolled his eyes.

"Says the man with zero fashion sense." I laughed.

"Perhaps, but I have common sense, and I'm not going to walk around in shoes all day that hurt my feet." He stated.

"Whatever." I playfully shoved him. "Are you hungry?"

"A little. What are you in the mood for?"

"I don't care." I shrugged. "What's around here?"

"Pizza, Chinese, Wings; just about anything." We paused.

"Wings?" I shrugged.

"Sounds good to me."

We sat down on the barstools at the table and ordered a couple drinks. Since Deuce was driving, I ordered a Long Island while he drank iced tea. We perused the menu and decided upon a basket of Caribbean Jerk wings.

The Long Islands went down smoothly. I had forgotten how easily they went down until I stood up to leave. I staggered just a bit and held onto the side of the chair.

"Woah." I giggled.

"Come on, drunk." Deuce took my arm and led me out of the restaurant.

"I'm fine." I leaned heavily against him as we made our way through the courtyard.

"Sure, you are." He rolled his eyes at me and laughed. "You are a cheap drunk."

"Thanks. You're so sweet."

Deuce helped me into the car and buckled me in. I rested my head back and took a deep breath. I felt so relaxed and excited. He climbed into the driver's seat of my car and started the engine.

"You know what I want to do tonight?" I turned towards him as we pulled out of the mall parking lot.

"What's that?" He kept his eyes on the road.

"Let's go to Vegas."

"Vegas? Tonight?" He glanced over at me. "Seriously?"

"Yeppers." I giggled. "Let's do it."

"I'm on call tomorrow." He stated as if that settled everything.

"It's only eight o'clock. We'll be back in time." I waved my hands drunkenly for emphasis. "Three hours there, three hours to play, three hours back. No problem."

"Arya. Be realistic. It's not possible." He chuckled. "We'll be there in less than a week. And we're not getting married tonight."

"Why not?" I teased him.

"Well, for starters we've talked about it, but I haven't proposed to you." Deuce smirked. "Are you proposing to me?"

"Nope. I've never proposed to anyone, and I'm not going to start now."

"I've never proposed to anyone either." He declared.

"You didn't propose to Cathy?"

"Nope. She proposed to me."

"And you were stupid enough to say yes."

"Don't be judging me your ex isn't exactly a prize."

"I'm not going to argue with you on that one. He's an arrogant prick." I rolled my eyes. "What about Amber? You never proposed to her."

"No. I thought about it. We talked about it. Thankfully, I saw what a heartless, cheating, bitch she was before I ever bought a ring." He explained.

"Well, that's good."

"True." He paused for a red light and kept his eyes forward.

I held my breath, waiting for him to say something, anything.

"Do you want to marry me?" Deuce asked.

"Do I?" I laughed, trying to figure out what his next move was.

"Well, do you?"

"We've discussed it."

"Yes."

"I thought we agreed we know we're going to do it eventually." I suddenly felt ridiculous through my drunken haze.

"We did." I could tell he was having fun toying with me.

He kept his eyes forward, giving me nothing to go on. I hated it when he did this; especially when my mind wasn't clear. He was enjoying watching me squirm.

"So ..." His voice trailed off. I shifted uncomfortably in my seat. "Will you marry me?" He glanced over at me with a sly smile.

"Yes, of course!" I laughed. "Are you serious?"

"You already said yes." He laughed. "So, yes, I'm serious."

"Are we engaged?" I stupidly asked, but none of it seemed real.

"I believe we are."

"Oh, my God." I muttered in stunned disbelief as he pulled in my parking spot and shut the car off. I couldn't believe this was happening. And this way.

I followed him up to my apartment, my mind clearing with each step. Thankfully, Brylee wasn't home. She must have been out with her friends. We headed straight to my room and closed the door behind us.

"Are we really engaged?" I sat down on the corner of my bed.

"Well, I asked you to marry me, and you said yes. So, yes. We're engaged." Deuce came over and sat down beside me, putting his hand over mine. "But we're not going to Vegas tonight."

"Are you saying that you want to get married next week while we're there?"

"Sure." He flopped back on the bed and made himself comfortable.

"You don't want a ceremony here with your family and friends?" I asked, stretching out beside him.

"No. Do you?"

"No. I did that before, and it was a disaster. Besides, none of my family is here except for Brylee. My parents and son wouldn't be able to come. At least not without substantial notice and I mean months. My son is in the military, and his schedule is out of his control." The realization was devastating. It was hard to fathom getting married without my family.

"So, why don't we get married in Vegas and then have a big reception after we buy a new house?" He asked.

"Okay." I squeaked. My head was beginning to spin, and it wasn't from the alcohol. "How would we do this? We have two homes. I don't want to live at your house, and there's not enough space for all of us here." I pointed out. "Hell, I haven't even seen your house!" I took a deep breath. I knew I was rambling, but I didn't care. "I haven't met your parents. You haven't met mine or my son and his family." I tried to laugh but snorted instead. "Let's not even mention the fact that this is completely crazy. We've known each other for less than two months!" Saying it out loud made it sound even more ludicrous then it did in my head.

"Have you ever seen the movie *When Harry Met Sally?*" Deuce asked as he pulled me to him.

"Of course." I rested my head on his chest. "It's one of my favorites."

"Well, you remember at the end of it when Billy Crystal finally realizes on New Year's Eve that he wants to spend his life with Meg Ryan. He chases her down to the party and proceeds to explain to her that when you realize who you want to spend the rest of your life with you want it to start right away." He leaned over and kissed the top of my head. "That's how I feel. Why should we wait? We know this is right. We know we're going to do it eventually, right?" He looked at me imploringly.

"Yes." I squeaked.

"Then why not do it now?"

"Okay. Let's get married in Vegas." I leaned up and kissed him excitedly.

I pulled his shirt up over this head and tossed it aside. I placed my hand on his bare chest. His muscles rippled under my touch. I ran my fingers lightly over the small amount of hair on his chest and smiled up into his eyes with a devilish grin. My fingers traced lightly over his warm skin.

Deuce's face took on a serious expression. He reached down and took my hands in his.

"Do you know what you are to me? You remember the scene from the *Deadpool* movie we saw where Ryan Reynolds was drowning, and on the other side of the barrier, the love of his life was sitting there waiting for him, trying to get to him — that is me. I was drowning, and you saved me. You are the love of my life; saving me from everything I have ever known. You are the light of my life." Deuce said softly as he held my face and looked lovingly into my eyes.

~

We kept that part of our little adventure a secret. Neither of us was sure how everyone was going to react but considering the short amount of time we'd been together we figured it wasn't going to be positive.

We set out after rush hour on Thursday morning. The desert sun was blazing down on us. We had the air conditioner on high, but the heat was still intense through the car windows.

We passed through the city and abruptly found ourselves on a two-lane highway surrounded by desert. There was nothing as far as the eye could see but cacti and buttes. I felt like I was in a foreign land. It was easy to see how someone could get lost in the desert.

We had one of those road trip drives where you talk about anything, everything, and nothing. We laughed, and we cried. Then we laughed some more. I confessed things to Deuce I had never shared with my best friend and he did the same. Our conversation was so intimate and personal. I felt closer to him than I had anyone before in my life.

Passing into Nevada over the Hoover Dam was exciting. I couldn't help but think of all the films that had scenes filmed here. It was surreal seeing it in person. Movies certainly did not give it the grandeur justice it deserved.

We hit the Vegas strip shortly after one in the afternoon. The traffic was horrific. We weren't going anywhere fast. Deuce's GPS kept telling him to make a right, but there was no right to turn. We were blocked by a concrete medium, so we circled around the block.

It took us another three tries around the block before we found a back alleyway to cut through to get to New York New York. The casino and hotel were larger than life. I could hear people screaming on the rollercoaster that ran throughout the building and the grounds as I climbed out of the car.

Deuce handed the keys to the valet and retrieved our bags from the car. He placed them on the cart and headed towards the front doors. I stood there a moment longer absorbing the ambiance.

This was going to be fun.

~

Deuce unlocked the door to our suite with his key card. He held the door open and let me pass into the room first. The suite was enormous. We had a sitting room, a table and chairs, a king-sized bed, and a jacuzzi tub to enjoy.

I unpacked my clothes and hung them up in the armoire. Deuce preferred to leave his things in his duffle bag. I didn't say anything to him about it but mentioned that he would be ironing his shirt tomorrow.

"Don't you know that's one of the perks of getting married?" He kissed my forehead. "I no longer have to iron my own clothes anymore." He smirked.

"If you think I'm going to turn into some laundress, you've got another thing coming, Mister." I laughed and poked him in the chest.

"Laundress, cook, maid. You can assume whatever title you prefer." He teased.

"How about lover, friend, partner in crime?" I suggested.

"I like that."

"What would you like to do first?" I sat down on the bed and stared up at him.

"You have a one-track mind, woman." He chuckled. "Why don't we shower, change, and go get some dinner?"

"Sounds good to me. I'm starving."

Deuce and I ate Shephard's Pie at an Irish pub at the casino. We consumed a couple drinks and decided to walk around. People watching along the Vegas strip was an experience every person should participate in at least once in their lifetime. It was an entirely different level of hilarity.

We walked into the MGM, doing some window shopping and browsing for souvenirs. We passed by a jewelry store, and Deuce squeezed my hand.

"Want to look for a ring?" He smiled.

"Um," I suddenly felt very uncomfortable. "Sure. I guess so."

"Aren't we going to need one to get married?" He nudged me playfully.

"Yeah, but," I hated this part.

Deuce and I did not discuss money. I had no idea what he made, nor did I care.

"But what?" He questioned and pulled me into the store.

"Fine."

The store was filled with a variety of jewels for men and women. They had rings, bracelets, necklaces, and watches, among other things. It was a beautiful selection. The overly stylish saleslady pounced on us as soon as we entered.

"Good evening. Is there anything special you're looking for?" She asked.

"No, just browsing." I said at the same time Deuce replied.

"A wedding ring."

I looked over at him and wanted to step on his foot or something to keep him quiet. I hated pushy salespeople.

"What kind of setting are you interested in?" She asked.

"Something plain and simple." Those four words immediately caused her to lose all interest in us. Thank goodness.

"What do you like?" Deuce asked as the lady drifted off to talk to another customer.

"What do you like?" I asked.

He was looking at wedding sets that were a bit more extravagant than what I had in mind.

"I was serious about something plain and simple." I walked over to the glass case of bands.

"Are you sure?" Deuce looked skeptical.

"I don't feel comfortable walking around with thousands of dollars on my finger. I'd be too scared." I confessed.

"Then what do you have in mind?"

"Something like this." I pointed to two thin white gold bands that fit together with a little dip in them. The front of both was covered with tiny little diamonds. It was simple and elegant. Exactly my style.

"Are you sure?" He asked once again.

"Absolutely."

"Okay," he motioned to the sales lady who seemed less than thrilled but opened the display case and handed me the rings. They were a bit loose. "Can these be resized before one tomorrow?"

"Of course." She smiled and measured my finger for the exact size.

"What do you think of this one?" I nudged Deuce and indicated a solid black ring in the men's display.

"I like that. Can we see that one also?" He inquired.

"Sure," She opened the display case and handed him the ring. "What size do you need?"

"I'm not sure." He shrugged.

She picked up the ring chart and checked his size. "I don't believe we have that size. Let me check in the back."

"Do you like that one?" I wanted him to be sure.

"Yeah. Don't you?"

"It suits you."

"We don't have it in your size, but I can order it." The saleslady smiled. "Or would you like to see something else? I'm not sure what we have in your size though."

"You and your fat fingers," I laughed.

"Sorry."

"Don't be sorry. I love them." I leaned into him and giggled.

"You're terrible."

"You love me." I smirked.

"Let's just order them." Deuce told the saleslady.

"Okay," She walked over to the computer and Deuce took care of everything.

"Wonderful. You can pick up her rings tomorrow after one, and we will mail yours to your home address." She handed Deuce the papers and receipt.

"Thank you," he stuffed the paperwork in his back pocket on our way out.

TWENTY-THREE

I WOKE UP IN THE oversized suite with Deuce lying naked on the pillow beside me. He was half on his stomach with his leg kicked up crooked beside me. He was snoring softly and looked so peaceful like a sleeping angel.

I carefully climbed out of bed so as not to disturb him. I crept into the power room to refresh myself and brush my teeth before he awoke. I ran the brush through my long blond hair until it gleamed in the light. I studied my face in the mirror. I had a golden tan that was offset by the bikini lines I adorned at the pool. Although I was blessed with resilient skin, and people told me I looked a decade younger than my age, I was still self-conscious of my appearance.

I crawled silently back into bed and kissed Deuce softly on the cheek. He stirred slightly and reached for me blindly. He drew me closer to him, wrapping his arm tightly around me; his body spooned up behind mine.

"Good morning." He whispered with his eyes still closed.

"Good morning, my love. Did you sleep well." I kissed his cheek once again.

"Yes. I love waking up beside you." A small smile spread across his lips.

"I do too. I love watching you sleep. You look so peaceful, like a little boy." I snuggled up against his warm body.

He laid there, holding me tightly in his arms. I closed my eyes and breathed in the scent of his skin. I loved the feel of his arms about me. I felt safe and secure; as if nothing in the world could ever harm me if I resided there.

Deuce ran his fingers lightly over the outside of my thigh causing gooseflesh to rise over my skin. He traced his fingertips over my hip along my side, resting on my breast. His featherlike touched toyed with my nipple making it stand erect before him. He brought his lips down to it and danced teasingly over it.

I nudged my buttocks against his large, hard cock. I could feel it throbbing pressed on my ass. I maneuvered myself to place him between my thighs and teased him gloriously. I absolutely loved tormenting him.

Deuce's sucking increased in intensity as he hungrily lapped at my breast. He shifted himself just enough to bring the head of his cock in between my lips. In one quick thrust, he entered me with such a force that it took my breath away.

Several strokes later, Deuce held my hips and rolled over upon his back; placing me in his second favorite position, a reverse cowgirl.

Deuce had incredible stomach muscles, and drove himself deeply into me as I leaned back, steadying myself up on my arms. His hands ran up from my hips to cup both my breasts. His fingers tweaked my nipples, sending electric shocks through my body.

I threw my head back and moaned loudly. Deuce pulled himself up and kissed the back of my neck as he drove himself deeper into me. His hand slid down my abdomen and parted my lips with his fingers. He began to vigorously rub my clitoris.

My breathing quickened as the intensity heightened and spread like fire throughout my body. I arched my back and let it ripple through me. I screamed out in ecstasy as I felt Deuce's muscles tightened beneath me as he reached climax and moaned loudly.

My body collapsed upon his, our breathing was labored. His hands wandered up my body and rested on my breast. He massaged them gently enjoyed the effect his torment was having on me. He kissed the nape between my shoulder and neck with such tenderness. Then, I felt his thick cock twitch inside me, causing my muscles to spasm involuntarily. Deuce giggled; he loved his petty torments.

"Stop that." I playfully smacked his thigh.

"What?" I could hear the smile in his voice as he tried to act innocent before doing it again.

"Damn it." I laughed a bit harder as my body had his intended reaction.

"I don't know what you're talking about." He tightened his grip and repeated his action. I tried to squirm off him, but he held me firmly while he continued laughing.

I fought against him, breaking free, but rolling around on the bed playfully wrestling. I couldn't imagine a better way to start the day.

After we showered and got dressed, we headed downstairs to catch an Uber ride to the county clerks office. It was a hot and miserable day. The noon sun blazed down upon us. The short ride was uncomfortable as the young driver wove in and out of mid-day traffic on the interstate through downtown Las Vegas.

Thankfully, we had completed our marriage application online, and it took the clerk only a couple minutes to issue us our marriage license. We smiled at each other as we happily signed our names and took the license with us for the Officiate.

We were less than five hours to becoming husband and wife.

Deuce and I dropped the paperwork off in our suite before we had lunch in a small restaurant off the casino. Afterward, we thought we'd browse the strip and pick up my rings before getting ready for our wedding. The butterflies in my stomach swarmed, and nothing I could say to myself was calming me down.

I was so nervous. I had no doubt about my love for Deuce or his for me. What terrified me was how quickly it had all transpired. I kept reminding myself of the words Deuce had said about being positive it would happen eventually, so why not do it now?

His little adage regarding the scene from *When Harry Met Sally* remained imprinted on my brain. Billy Crystal claiming at the end of the movie that when he realized what he wanted for the rest of his life, he wanted it to start immediately, was being replayed every two minutes by my overly panicked brain.

"Would you look at the size of those?" His voice broke my train of thought.

"Is that a drink?" I chuckled at the three-foot hourglass shaped drinking glass.

"You'd be hammered after finishing one of those."

"I could use that today." I smiled and playfully nudged him.

"Then I'll get you one." He grinned down at me. "I'm not taking the chance of you backing out on me."

"No chance of that." The words came straight from my heart, and I meant them, but my mind was ready to sprint for the door at break-neck speeds.

We walked up to the counter and looked over the wide range of drinks they offered for that glass. I shouldn't have been, but I was shocked when I saw the price tag for it — $56.00.

"No. Wait. Deuce, that's ridiculous." I exclaimed.

"It's Vegas." He shrugged casually. "You like Long Island's, right?" I nodded, and he proceeded to talk to the bartender.

"It's outrageous what they charge for things here, isn't it?" a couple about the same age as us, had walked up beside me.

"Yes, it is." I agreed.

"It's Vegas." The man shrugged. "We saved up to take a special honeymoon, and everything is twice what we thought it was." He smiled.

"Well, congratulations." I told them.

"Are you two married?" She asked.

"We will be in a couple hours." I told them.

"Liquid strength?" He asked with a small laugh.

"I hope so." I admitted.

"Well, congratulations to you both as well. I'm sure you'll be very happy."

"Thank you, you too." Deuce handed me the oversized beverage, and we stepped aside for the other couple to place their order.

We browsed our way through Caesar Palace. The shops were breathtaking, and the garments and bobbles were astounding. I was in pure shopper's heaven. Thankfully, I had Deuce there to put a curb on my appetite.

The drink was very potent. It didn't take long for the effects to go straight to my head. I began holding onto Deuce's arm not simply as a sign of affection, but also to maintain my balance.

By the time we'd made it back to the New York New York, my drink was more than three-quarters of the way gone. We slide into the slots area, and the waitress promptly took our drink orders. Deuce ordered a rum and Coke, I another Long Island. When she set the drinks down beside us, he took a long sip of his before pulling the handle once again on the slot machine. Once she was out of sight, dumped my new drink into my existing one and took another long sip of it.

Two hundred dollars ahead, we returned to our room to shower and get ready to head to the chapel.

~

Our idiot Uber driver twisted around the backroads of Vegas trying to get us to the chapel on time. We were set to be married in 10 minutes, but traffic was horrific. We finally arrived at the Graceland Wedding Chapel five minutes after our ceremony was set to begin.

"Are you ready?" Deuce opened the car door and offered me his hand.

"My mom used to tell me I'd be late for my own wedding." I laughed, holding his hand as I climbed out of the car. "I hope she never finds out she was right."

The man at the counter quickly checked us in and handed me a rose bouquet of flowers and a rose for me to pin on Deuce's shirt. The couple getting married after us were already waiting their turn, but graciously agreed to wait a few extra minutes for us. They were wearing matching Dr. Seuss's shirts from *The Cat in the Hat* with Elvis wigs. They were a comical sight.

The clerk showed us were to take our places and introduced us to the photographer. Deuce stood up by the altar while Elvis and I stood back at the entrance. The music started, and Elvis began signing *Can't Help Falling in Love* as we began our descent down the aisle. When we reached Deuce, Elvis handed him the microphone where Deuce proceeded to sing the song to me. I could not contain my laughter. I was shocked by how well he sang, and he was such a good sport in playing his part. It would forever be our song.

Elvis performed the ceremony, and we giggled our way through it. The Long Islands had done their job on me. I was surprised I was still standing with the amount of alcohol I had consumed before our arrival. Thankfully my strappy heels were blunt and not stiletto, or I would have certainly broken my ankle by this point.

We posed for several pictures afterward, each of us had a plastered grin across our faces. I believe we were both still in shock that we actually did it. We were married — for better or for worse, it was done now.

We stumbled out of the chapel, half intoxicated and high on life. And partially stunned with disbelief. We took an Uber back to the casino to change clothes. We were both starved and realized we hadn't eaten since breakfast.

Our reception dinner was spent at a small diner where we ate pulled pork and coleslaw barbeque. The air was muggy, and my buzz was wearing off quicker than I would have liked. I sipped another Long Island trying to ward off the headache that brewing on the outskirts of my brain.

Deuce and I walked hand in hand down to Treasure Island to check out the show. We snapped silly photos in front of the ships and Señor Frog's. We lost twenty dollars in the slots while downing a couple more drinks.

We stopped in front of the fountains at the Bellagio. There were scores of people gathered along the sidewalks and leaning on the concrete railing. We stopped amongst them when we heard Cher belting out her song; *Do You Believe in Love*. The fountains began their synchronized dance to the music.

I pulled out my cell and turned on the video screen and began recording. I edged my way through the crowds to improve my view. Deuce was standing about three feet from me. I could hear his muffled laughter and finally turned to see what was so funny.

Deuce was nestled in the corner of an inlet. His shoulders were rocking from laughter. His arms were crossed, and he had a hand over his mouth, trying to keep control of himself. I glanced over at him, trying to figure out what was so funny.

He stuck out his index finger beneath his nose, indicating the gentleman a few feet to the right of him. My eyes immediately followed. The feminine middle-aged man had his eyes closed, lost in the music and was dancing wildly in his navy-blue slacks, dress shoes, and buttoned-down blue dress shirt. He looked like every other professional male, except for her outwardly feminine dance movements.

Despite myself, I busted out laughing. Unfortunately, I wasn't nearly as subtle as Deuce, and the man's eyes flew open. He looked directly at me and turned four shades of red. His dancing immediately ceased. Deuce grabbed my arm and moved me further down the sidewalk away from the man; giggling all the way.

We stumbled our way through the Bellagio, the Venetian, and several others as we made our way down the strip towards New York New York. We stopped and played at various ones having drinks and enjoying having not one responsibility in the world. That would come on Sunday.

~

Sunday morning, I relaxed back against the soft, plush, luxury bed duvet and closed my eyes. My new husband was sleeping soundly beside me. His arm rested across my chest, and his leg was tossed over me carelessly. His soft and steady breathing was like a lullaby. I reached over and ran my fingers lightly through his hair. I was completely and utterly in love with this man.

I loved the way Deuce explored my body without reservation or hesitation. With him, sex was fun, it was playful, it was adventurous; it was breathtakingly passionate. Every time we were together was like the first time. We could never get enough of each other. There was always that burning fire, that unbelievable desire, the unquenchable thirst that if I died tomorrow, I would die with unbridled happiness.

But my children. What would they say?

~

Four days and three nights in Las Vegas changed our lives forever and marked the beginning of a new journey. Deuce checked us out of the hotel while I waited with our luggage for the valet to bring my car around.

I stood on the curb wearing a red, soft, spaghetti strapped, high-low dress, my strappy sandals, big floppy hat, and dark sunglasses. My four-day drinking binge was coming to an end, and now I was paying dearly for it.

Deuce leaned over and kissed me gently on the cheek. The valet popped the trunk and helped Deuce load our bags. I grimaced in the sunlight as I climbed into the car. I dreaded the long drive back to Phoenix.

Deuce closed the trunk and tipped the valet before climbing into the car. He put the car in drive and eased up onto the strip. He reached over and took my hand in his.

"Well, Mrs. Steglich, what now?"

AUTHOR BIOGRAPHY

Addison Winters, otherwise known as A. L. Waddington, has a master's in psychology and is currently completing her doctorate. She is the author of the bestselling *EVE* series and *With Honors* series and the new *Spirit Quest* series and *Heat of Arrest* series. When she's not buried in research, reading or lost is a world of her own creation, she enjoys gardening, hiking in the Arizona mountains, and spending time with her family and friends. Addison lives in Arizona with her husband Eric, their daughters, and the terror twin puppies.

Find out more about Addison Winters and her works at alwaddington.com.

This little tryst will never survive past college—but Alex is determined to enjoy it the fullest while it lasts.

MAKING THE DEAN'S LIST, BOOK 2

In an ideal world, the right man comes along, you fall madly in love, and live happily ever after. But real life isn't quite so simple, and timing is everything!

And having to choose between two charismatic, sexy, and compassionate men isn't easy...the fact that they are father and son puts a new degree of complications into the mix. How do you decide between the boy you're currently dating and the man you know you could spend the rest of your life with...if you'd only met him first?

Welcome to Alex's world. Balancing a full-time career as a college student and being a full-time single parent is all she believed she would have to contend with when she decided to go back to school. But she began a little tryst with a fellow student that turned into so much more. And then she met his father...

Sexual escapades, student teaching, homework, her children's activities, the annoying ex-husband, and friends who wish they could switch places with her keep Alex's life interesting. But the problem with seeing two men is that eventually, the truth comes out. Will she follow her heart, or will she forego her own desires and play it safe?

Don't miss out on a sneak peek at the final installment in the With Honors series, Transferring Credits, Book 3.

TRANSFERRING CREDITS, BOOK 3

Confrontation. Alienation. Truth.

The cards are on the table, and everyone has shown their hand. And no one is innocent. No one is coming out without a few scars.

Alex, Mason, and Hayden must face the consequences for their actions and deal with the fallout for the decisions they've made. But are they ready? Can they handle the reception they are about to receive from their friends and family? When the dust finally settles, can they look at each other?

In the gripping conclusion of the With Honors series, Alex must decide once and for all between Mason and Hayden. But will her decision destroy two families? Will she be able to let go of one of the two men she has grown to love and cherish? And will she be able to live with herself?